WARNING

This book contains sexually explicit scenes and adult language. It may be considered offensive to some readers. This book is for sale to adults ONLY.

* * * * * * * * * * * * * * * * * *

Please store your files wisely where they cannot be accessed by underage readers.

ISBN-13: 978-1987863505
ISBN-10: 198786350X

Other books by Shyla Starr:

<u>Persuasive Billionaire BWWM Romance Series</u>

Stacey is trying to keep a handle on her life the best that she can. She is on the verge of losing her job and her apartment, while taking care of her sick grandmother. Her life takes an unexpected turn when she meets Charlie, who works for the construction company that is attempting to persuade her to move out of her home.

<u>Tenacious Billionaire BWWM Romance Series</u>

Adalia is too proud to accept help from the billionaire playboy, Trent Dawson. How long can she maintain her resolve? The bank is at her heels to repossess her business. To make matters worse, Adalia finds suspicious evidence of Trent's philandering ways. She must determine whether to trust Trent with the fate of her business and her heart.

<u>Elusive Billionaire Romance Series</u>

Billionaire Hendrick is trying to repair his company's image by putting in some volunteer work, building a school and hospital for the impoverished children in Africa. There, he meets a beautiful African American volunteer, Jocelyn. They hit it off right away but does she belong in his world?

<u>Ardent Billionaire Romance Series</u>

Deirdre doesn't know what to make of the gorgeous man that seems to be interested in her. His name is Parker Walters and he seems friendly enough. There is just something off about him. Why is he trying the hide the fact that he is the heir to his father's billion dollar software empire?

Fervent Billionaire BWWM Romance Series

Alexandra had never been with a white man before. She had seen William at the café before but she always kept her distance. It was unfortunate that their first chance meeting happened when she dropped her breakfast and spilled coffee all over his expensive business suit.

Audacious Billionaire BWWM Romance Series

Chante is torn between staying close to a man beyond her league, and fleeing from him to spare herself from a hopeless position. But she finds she is propelled into a place where she needs to confront her doubts and cast her fate aside to follow the dictates of her heart. Damned if she does and miserable is she doesn't, how will Chante face the events that will lead her to a place of pure happiness or to the pits of a broken heart?

Get the latest update on new releases from the author at:

https://shylastarr.com/newsletter/

This book contains all the stories of the "Lonely Billionaire Romance Series"

1 - Love Anew

Tricia was hired to care for billionaire John's wife, who is dying. An unlikely romance emerges after his wife, Rebecca, gives John permission to pursue his happiness after she is gone.

2 - Love Bound

Tricia found herself in another caretaking role. This time, the patient would be her own mother. Her relationship with John was getting complicated. She didn't know whether their feelings for each other were genuine or part of the grieving process from the death of John's wife after a long period of illness. By immersing herself with the task of taking care of her mother, her hope was to forget about John and move on with her life. It didn't hurt that Tricia's best friend's brother, Rod, was a successful and attractive distraction.

3 - Love Decided

John shows up at Tricia's doorstep to finish what they had started. Unsure of what to do but still having real feelings for him, she accepts his invitation for dinner. While at the rodeo with John, Tricia bumps into Rod, the man that she has started to develop feelings for. With two men vying for her affection, Tricia is left with a difficult decision.

Lonely Billionaire Romance Series

Books One to Three

By Shyla Starr

Table of Contents

Book One

Chapter One

TRICIA REACHED for another blanket. "Are you cold?" she asked.

Rebecca's breath was raspy as she responded. As her lungs shut down due to ALS, or Amyotrophic Lateral Sclerosis, her ability to speak had started to decline. Muscle by muscle, ALS targeted the body and made it impossible for the individual to live a normal life. It had started a few years ago with Rebecca's legs. Now, her lung muscles were starting to freeze as well. Tricia winced as she thought about the future. If Rebecca chose to use machines to stay alive, her entire body would eventually stop working. At some point, her mind would remain functioning and she would be locked into her body.

Rebecca managed to squeeze out a feeble yes. Reaching over to the cupboard, Tricia removed a blanket and carefully tucked her in. Tricia had spent years training to be a nurse and really liked her job. Since she was an excellent nurse, she had caught the eye of the billionaire, John, at one of the couple's many trips to hospitals around the country. He had noticed the love and care she took with each patient. After a moment's hesitation, Tricia had allowed him to convince her to take care of his wife.

Pictures of Rebecca dotted the room. Since she was unable to leave, John had striven to make her room look like favorite memories of her life and activities. A young, healthy Rebecca smiled in each photo. In the few years she had been physically active, she had acquired awards for horseback riding, cooking and other projects. Now, though, this time of physical fitness had passed. Instead of dashing through the fields on her favorite horse, Rebecca spent her time in this room. She had taken her difficulties in stride and was truly brave in the face of all of these medical issues.

Finishing with the blanket, Rebecca started to say something. Leaning closer to hear her, Tricia finally pulled up a chair. "What do you need, Rebecca?" she queried.

Sighing, Rebecca whispered, "I need to talk to John. I have to tell him how I want to die."

Squeezing her hand, Tricia nodded. "Once I leave your room, I will go get him. Just in case he is not around, did you want me to give him a message?"

Rebecca tried to nod, but her head did not respond all the way. "Yes, I do. You need to tell him that I do not want any machines. He could keep me alive forever with a breathing tube, but I do not want to live a life where I am permanently locked into my body. And," she paused and struggled to take another breath. "I do not want him to stop enjoying life or waiting around for my eventual death. If God wants to take my soul now, we should not interfere."

Tricia nodded sadly. Most patients with ALS were more afraid of being stuck within their minds than actual death. She understood, but she could not imagine what life would be like without Rebecca's gentle soul. "I will tell him," she said.

Leaving the room, Tricia traversed the hallways of the mansion. John had built his fortune by buying and selling real estate properties. His initial money had arrived through an early investment in the dot com boom before the bubble burst. After seeing the dangers of the stock market, he had started to just buy and rent out properties. Even with the recent recession, he still made a profit. Instead of selling his properties or developing, he had continued to rent them out. In a decade or two, he had talked of selling and retiring. His plans had arrived before his wife had been diagnosed with ALS. Unwilling to speak of his life after her future death, Tricia had not asked about any change in his future plans.

The halls of the house were dotted with white oak doorways that led to a myriad of rooms. Plush white carpet softly surrounded Tricia's feet as she walked. She dreaded the conversation that was about to happen. Every day, she updated John about the status of his wife. Unfortunately, she seldom had good news to share. She nodded to John's secretary as she entered the office. Unlike most rich men, he used a male secretary. Before talking had become so difficult, Rebecca had explained that he tried to hire primarily males so that Rebecca would never worry about his fidelity. Since Tricia was intended to cater just to his wife, she had been allowed to work there despite her gender.

Knocking on the door, she heard a sound in the room and assumed that he was telling her to come in.

She entered the office and John motioned for her to sit down. His tousled brown hair fell softly across his face and his icy blue eyes were focused intently on paperwork in front of him. Between running an empire and worrying about his wife, he seldom took time any more for his personal appearance. His face was growing a rugged stubble and looked like it had not seen a razor for a while. Dashing and muscular, his good looks had an almost otherworldly level of gorgeousness. John was known among business associates for his confidence and aggressive tactics. He played fair, but he managed his company with the best of his abilities. Sitting down in a dark brown leather chair, Tricia waited for him to finish reading his paperwork. Dark hues and gold glinted throughout the old-fashioned room. She glanced around and noticed that he had installed a new marble bust of Benjamin Franklin. As she waited, Tricia pondered this piece of information. For the most part, she only talked about Rebecca with John. They had carefully avoided any other topic. She wondered what made Benjamin Franklin so special. Before she could ponder his personality or secret likes anymore, John looked up from the paperwork.

"How is she?" he asked. His eyes had the dull look in them that came when people had given up hope. John knew that Rebecca would not be getting better.

"As well as expected. Her speech is deteriorating as her lung function slows. She told me today that she wanted to make arrangements about how she dies."

John sighed. "Do you know what she wants? I will go see her shortly."

"I think she wants to tell you when she wants to die. She does not want to develop locked-in syndrome and does not want to be kept alive by machines." Tricia looked down so he could have a moment to process the news.

"I assumed as much. Damn, Rebecca is probably more worried about me than she is about her. She is absolutely convinced that keeping her on machines will ruin my life." John cursed under his breath. Although he was the pillar of strength and decisive action in his professional life, he always expressed tenderness when even the name of his wife was brought up.

Tricia tried to phrase her response. He needed to understand that it was up to Rebecca. "I think that may be part of it, sir, but it is not the whole story. She also does not want to live that way. You cannot just keep her close to you because you love her. If she does not want to be artificially kept alive, you will have to let her have her way, sir."

John's eyes glimmered in amusement. "It isn't often that my decisions are questioned. What makes you so brave, Tricia? Grown men seldom stand up to me and you seem to make a habit of it." He smiled warmly and Tricia knew that the comment was meant genuinely.

She shrugged. As she moved her shoulders, her dark black hair swished slightly at her back. Born into a ghetto in Dallas, she had been raised in the black community. Working for a billionaire was a far different experience, but she had learned to stand up for herself from her grandmother. Energetic and vocal, her grandmother still controlled family decisions into her 90s. "I only care about your wife. She is not strong enough to put the energy into standing up for herself. It is my job to represent her interests and I don't care who you are."

John laughed at her frankness and stood up. Straightening her jacket, he pressed his hand against the small of her back as he led her out of the office. "Well, then, why don't you come with me? You are right that I care about my wife a great deal. Having such a vocal supporter and a loving friend will make this easier for her." His hand stayed on the small of her back longer than necessary. Instead of pulling away, she let him. She knew it was wrong to hope, but she had found herself wishing that... well, that something would happen. Not now, but someday. Her mother would kill her for bringing home a white guy, but she had started to feel a growing attraction for John over the last few years. Deep down, she thought he may feel the same way. She knew that he went out of his way to avoid her when she was at the mansion. He took every step possible to remove himself from a temptation that was so obvious.

Following Tricia down the hallway, John averted his eyes from looking at her. Her cocoa brown skin was complemented perfectly by a slim-fitting red dress. As she walked, her hips swayed just slightly enough for him to imagine what it would be like to have her hips swaying on top of him. John forced himself more to look away. Throughout his wife's illness he had been celibate. Early on, Rebecca had lost the ability to have sex. Although he tried to convince himself that his fascination with Tricia was just his celibate life, he knew that it was more than that. Feeling guilty, he started to think about how the conversation with his wife would go.

Entering the room, John smiled warmly at Rebecca and went over to kiss her head. He sat down in the chair next to her bed and held her hand gently. "So what is it that Tricia has been telling me? You want to talk about how you will die?" he said softly.

"Yes, dear. I do not want to be kept alive with machines. If you need something artificial to keep me alive, just let me go. I love you, but that is what I want." She waited for him to say something. In the background, Tricia remained quiet.

John tried to stay calm. He had put off thinking about her potential death for so long. "Are you sure that is what you want to do? I will be with you and love you forever, just say the word."

Rebecca closed her eyes. "I don't want that. When my time comes, let me go. Afterward, go on to live your life fully and take advantage of every chance that you have. Be happy. Live a full life. I enjoyed every moment of my life. Just let me sign the paperwork while I still can so that my wishes can be fulfilled."

With tears in his eyes, John leaned over Rebecca and kissed her hand. Holding her hand to his lip, he nodded. "Okay, I will make everything possible. Just let me get the lawyer here and we will figure it all out." He looked over at Tricia. "May I have a moment with my wife? Don't worry about waiting, I will make her dinner tonight and take care of her."

Tricia nodded and stepped out of the room. Walking to the kitchen, she sat down while the chef made her something to eat before she went home. Unaccustomed to living in staff housing on-site like the other servants and workers, Tricia had been rented an apartment nearby by John. She still chose to eat with the rest of the staff in the kitchen because it made her evenings less lonely. In addition, her rough upbringing had taught her the value of saving money. If John was willing to pay for all of his staff members, she was ready to eat.

Sitting at the counter, Tricia watched the cook work. "How is your family doing, Stuart?" she asked.

The cook smiled. He had twin daughters and loved to talk about them. "They are great. Their mother is going crazy though. They found some of the leftover spaghetti in the fridge and had a food fight." He chuckled and spooned some lasagna onto Tricia's plate. "Are you heading home after this?"

Tricia nodded as she took a bite. "John's going to stay with her tonight."

Stuart's face took on a gloomier note as he asked. "That poor man. And his wife... such a sweet lady. I don't know how you have the patience to do your job."

Handing him the plate, Tricia shrugged. "It helps people. Anything that makes the world better is worth doing. You should know—you make people happy as soon as they try a bite of your food."

Smiling, Stuart shooed her away. "You head home! No more of your flattery around here. Drive safe, Tricia."

Chapter Two

Exiting the building, Tricia nodded to the two guards at the entrance. Getting to know the staff had taken a long time. Most of the staff members had worked with John for at least a decade and were like a close-knit family. Although the first few months were hard, they had finally learned to accept her. She loved working with them and had gotten to know the intricate details of their lives.

Tricia drove home, showered, and started to prepare for bed. Today had been heart wrenching, but tomorrow would be better. She would get to see John for a brief moment again and spend another day helping Rebecca live a comfortable life.

After helping Rebecca fall asleep, Tricia started to head back to John's office. It was time for another daily meeting. Over the last few days, a flurry of paperwork had passed through the sick room as Rebecca completed her last wishes. Finally, it seemed like all of the paperwork was complete and Rebecca could finish her last days in peace. Knocking on the door, Tricia heard a noise inside and assumed that she was allowed to come in. Inside, John was bent over the desk and looked like he was crying. Tricia was not sure what to do for a moment. Should she leave and give him his privacy? Or should she hang around and offer him some comfort?

With all of her years working with sick people, she could not help wanting to go to him.

Stepping quietly across the room, she pulled up a chair next to John and gave him a hug. At first, he reacted with surprise. He had not realized how late it was in the day and did not expect to see anyone in his office.

"I..." he choked back some tears and did his best to calm down. "I am sorry, you should not have to see me like this."

Tricia shook her head. "You are only human. If I did not see you like this at least once, I'd be worried. Here, put your head on my shoulder."

Weakly, John obliged. His strength and confidence had vanished for the moment and all he could think about was the impending loss of his wife. Putting his head on her shoulder, he slowly let his tears dry up on their own. Tricia ran her hands through his hair gently to help soothe him.

The warmth of Tricia's body had a soothing effect on John. Her hair smelled like an intoxicating mix of lilacs and jasmine. Lifting his head up, John looked up into her eyes. Her lips were only a short distance away from his mouth. As he looked into her eyes, he realized that she was experiencing the same emotion. The professionalism she normally displayed had disappeared for a moment and he saw the naked desire that so perfectly mirrored his own. Gently, he kissed her lips. As she started to kiss him back, he sat back in his chair and pulled her onto him. She could feel his cock grow hard beneath her as she ran her fingers along his neck.

Tricia pulled back. "What are we doing?" she asked.

John shook his head. "I have no clue, but I can't stop. I've wanted this for so long." With that, he pulled her against him. After the rising sexual tension over the last few weeks, being held against his skin felt so right. She ran her hand along his shirt and started to unbutton it. He pulled off his suit jacket and shirt before reaching to pull off her shirt as well. Grasping her breast in his hand, he held his lips to her nipple and bit it until the nipple became hard. Moaning slightly, he reached for her pants to undo them. Ripping her pants from her body, he turned her over on the desk. Standing behind her, he entered her with one sharp thrust. Tricia closed her eyes as a wave of pleasure washed over her body. He had more than one reason to be confident. The entire shaft could not fit inside her, despite his deep thrusts into her body. Holding on to the edge of the desk, she pushed her body back into his. Waves of heat rolled off their bodies as they pushed toward climax. Faster and faster, he drove into her body until she started to orgasm. The clenching of her muscles and moans caused him to reach the brink and he came explosively inside of her. Falling on top of her on the desk, he held her chocolate skin in his ivory white arms.

Turning her over, he started to massage her breasts again. He ran his fingers down her body and started to finger her. After coming just a few moments before, her body was sensitive to any touch. Tricia let out a sigh of pleasure as he started to finger her again. As her moans grew in volume, John started to become harder again. He spread her legs on the top of the desk and pulled them around him. Thrusting into her again, he pushed deeply into her. For the moment, all they could think about was one another. After the sexual passion of the first orgasm, this time felt more like love or something similar. It felt like their bodies and souls had passed a whole lifetime just waiting for the other. Instead of the awkwardness of a new sexual partner, it felt like they had been together all along. Driving harder inside her, John orgasmed. His body shook as he released all of his pent up sexual energy inside of her. He moved toward the chair and pulled her body with him. Still inside of her, her legs were spread across him on the leather chair. Tricia kissed down the side of his body as she rocked her hips gently on top of him. He groaned with pleasure and agony as she moved on top of his member. Still sensitive from sex, it was his turn to experience heightened sensations. She moved her hips against him like a mad woman as she came closer and closer to orgasm. Tricia could feel it coming closer, but the orgasm just remained slightly out of reach. Finally, she felt it blossoming in her. Her body convulsed as she fell on top of him. Grabbing her cheeks, he pulled her hard against his body so that his full length was inside of her. Gasping with pleasure, she fell against his body and he held her in his arms.

For several long moments, they sat together naked on the chair. John lazily ran his hand along her back. Pulling her head up to look at him, he kissed her again. Their tongues moved in a type of gentle harmony before Tricia pulled away.

"What have we done?" she whispered softly. Guilt was starting to creep into the corners of her mind. She held him closer with the knowledge that this moment was about to end.

"I don't know. Do you regret it?" John asked quietly as he ran his fingers along her spine.

Tricia shrugged. "I really don't know. You are right. I have wanted this for so long, but... it just seems wrong. I know your wife wants you happy and cannot have sex with you. It still seems like we betrayed her in some way."

John kissed her forehead and lifted her off of him. Still hard, he emerged from her body. At the sight of him, Tricia started to feel turned on again. Struggling to focus, she turned to put on her clothes.

Slipping on his pants, John grabbed Tricia by the wrist for another long kiss. Despite her reservations, she did not want to stop. "Tricia, I have no clue what is right or wrong right now. All I know is that I was just happy. For the first time in years, I was able to be happy again and with you. Did you enjoy it?"

Tricia smiled and her brilliant white teeth formed a strikingly beautiful contrast with the rich darkness of her face. "Yes, of course I did. I just think that we should be careful not to let this happen again. While your wife is alive, it feels like we are betraying her. I like Rebecca and cannot just be the other woman."

John nodded. Taking her arm, he walked her to the door of his office. "Well, then, we shall have to control ourselves."

Tricia paused for a second. Confused, John waited and then realized what she was waiting for. "It's okay, you can go home for tonight. I'll take care of Rebecca."

As the office door shut, Tricia slid down against the wall until she was crouching on the floor. Thankfully, the secretary was gone for the day. Holding her head in her hands, she tried to think. How could she have let her desires get the best of her? She had an excellent job, a great salary and had finally been accepted by the staff. If anyone else knew about today, it would bring into question how she got the job. Despite her worries, she knew that she could never have chosen another option. Inexplicably, she had wanted him. Previous boyfriends had never brought her to that state of arousal or brought her past the line of right and wrong. Sitting there, Tricia decided that she would just do her best to forget that this happened. She had a job to do and this would only be a distraction.

Chapter Three

Despite the bustling throughout the mansion, everyone was walking in silence. A pall of death hung over the household as Rebecca lay close to her last moments. In the sickroom, Tricia stayed with Rebecca's hand clasped between her two palms. Stroking the fingertips, Tricia asked her if she needed anything.

"No," she rasped out slightly. "Just you. Thank you for staying with me." Her breath came out in brief shudders as she struggled to breathe. Tricia had already called the doctor, but he had not arrived yet.

After taking a few more breaths, Rebecca started to talk again. "Tricia, Tricia, can I ask you..." Her voice trailed off again as she struggled to breath.

Tricia nodded. "Ask me anything. I will do anything to help."

Rebecca took another breath. "Make sure John is happy. Promise me. He can't let my death hang over his life." She breathed again. "He focuses on his work too much. Make sure he takes time to enjoy life."

Patting her hand reassuringly, Tricia nodded. "I will do everything I can. You do not have to worry about anything, Rebecca."

They sat in silence for a few moments as Rebecca struggled to breathe. Tricia's thoughts raced as she tried to think of anything that would make these few moments easier. Pain medication had already been given, but it did not seem to help very much. For some of her patients, death was a welcome and easy experience. They slipped out of the world far easier than they had entered it. With ALS, death was a hoped-for and welcome end to the pain and boredom of the body breaking down. As she tried to consider what else to do, John burst into the room with the doctor close at his heels. His eyes had a crazed look in them and his hair was even more tousled than normal. A fastidious dresser, he was wearing a flannel shirt with dress slacks. Tricia stood up so that he could take the chair.

"Darling, I have the doctor. He will do whatever he can to help." He leaned closer and whispered something in Rebecca's ear in a quiet voice that was too low for the other people in the household to catch.

The doctor stepped up to the bed and placed his stethoscope on Rebecca's chest. Hiding his sadness, he adopted a patient and caring bedside manner. "Well, it is about as well as can be expected, my dear."

Rebecca struggled to speak. "Then…when... will I die?"

Pausing for a moment, the doctor looked at John.

John shook his head. "Don't worry. Go ahead and tell her what she wants to know. My wife would rather know when she will meet with death than pretend that everything will be okay."

Clearing his throat, the doctor averted his eyes. In a quiet voice, he started to speak. "Well, if I were to guess, I would estimate within the next 24 hours. Possibly tonight. Her lungs are unable to work like they are supposed to. Without enough oxygen, she will die. I can put her on a ventilator if you want."

"No," Rebecca spoke up. Her voice was the clearest it had been in days. "No ventilator."

John nodded in agreement. "I promised her that I would not keep her alive on machines. I will keep my promise, doctor."

The doctor nodded. He pulled out a vial of pills and set them on the night table. "In that case, you can give her this medication to ease the pain. If she cannot swallow them, you can grind them into a powder and mix them with water. Call me if you need anything else. At this point, there is nothing I can do other than ease the pain or put her on the ventilator." Saying goodbye to Rebecca, the doctor took his leave from John and left.

Chapter Four

The room was completely silent for a few moments after the doctor had gone away. John finally turned to Tricia and started to speak in a controlled, even voice. "Tricia, can you let me stay with my wife? Get something to eat from the kitchen and relax. If I need you, I will send one of the servants."

Tricia nodded and left the room. As she walked to the kitchen, noises were finally heard amid the silence. In the kitchen, all of the servants sat idly around the table. Casseroles and noodles dotted the table, but no one had the heart to eat anything.

Stuart turned to Tricia. His face was gloomier than she had ever seen it. "How is she? Is there any hope?"

Rather than give them false hope, Tricia just shook her head. "There is no way she will be able to recover from this. Rebecca probably has the night and maybe part of tomorrow to live. After that, she will be in God's hands."

One of the maids nodded. "It is probably for the best. The poor woman has gone through enough pain. I do not know how she does it."

Stuart pulled out some beers from the cabinet and started to pour a drink for everyone at the table. "Instead of sitting in silence, let's hold our own wake for Rebecca. Drink to her life instead of her death." He paused. "I think she would like that."

Slowly, everyone at the table lined up for their drink. Sitting around, they started to tell stories of Rebecca one by one. Before long, laughter started to flow through the room as the staff remembered the last several decades spent with her. As they tossed back some more beer, Stuart began to tell his favorite story about Rebecca. Laughing uncontrollably now, none of the staff members noticed when John walked in. He stood back against the wall for a few moments and listened to them talk. Finally, Tricia saw him. She immediately stopped laughing and fell silent. As if on cue, everyone else noticed her silence and did the same.

Before they could apologize, John held up his hand. "Don't stop, I think she will appreciate this. I just wanted to grab something to eat and bring upstairs with me. I will tell her about your wake and it should bring a smile to her lips." He smiled wanly. "God knows that she needs it."

Stuart nodded and then awkwardly resumed his story. He filled a plate for John. Afterward, John returned upstairs to stay with Rebecca.

Chapter Five

Several days had passed since Rebecca's death. Although they were depressed that she was gone, the staff members were also relieved that she was no longer suffering. The impromptu wake had left them with the indelible impression of the best memories of her and her life. Today, the entire staff was preparing the house for a reception after the funeral. The fridge was filled with food and each household member was dressed in black. Some of the servants were already at the church and were working on preparing the church.

Tricia hummed slightly as she got into her car. Although she was still gloomy about Rebecca, she was also relieved that her suffering was over. So far, she had even managed to keep her job. With all of the bustling about for the funeral, she had been working as an extra maid and cook around the house. Pulling into the funeral home, she went inside. As she entered, she smelled the overwhelming scent of flowers. Everywhere in the room, flowers had been placed.

Walking up to one of the maids, Tricia tapped her on the shoulder. "Sorry to bother you, but what can I do to help?"

The maid shrugged in response. "Ask John. I think he is behind the church in the garden."

Nodding, Tricia stepped out of the church and approached the garden. Rows of hedges surrounded a bench in back and a short trail. Now that she was looking for John, she had started to feel apprehensive. They had not spent any time alone together since having sex. In the last week, she had barely even seen him.

She finally was close enough to see the bench. John sat alone on the bench with a book. As she came closer, he looked up and patted the seat next to him. "Here, Tricia, come and sit with me for a moment."

Feeling awkward, she sat down next to him. She bit her lip and tried to think of something to say. "How are you doing, John?" she asked as she cursed herself for such an inelegant response.

John smiled. After so much turmoil, it felt strange to see him smile. Again, Tricia found herself thinking about how attractive he was. "I am doing fine. Everything is in order and I am just gathering my thoughts for a moment."

"I can leave if you want." She started to get up, but John grabbed her by the wrist. The simple touch set her blood on fire. Inexplicably, she wanted him right now. She glanced up into his eyes and saw that the same thought was passing through his mind. Instead of waiting to say something or asking permission, he held her wrist tightly and made her follow him deeper into the garden area. Surrounded by trees and bushes, they were finally alone. Pulling her into his arms, he started to kiss her slowly and passionately.

She pulled away slightly. "But what about the others?" she whispered.

"Don't worry about them. We have several hours and this spot is far enough out of the way that no one will be able to find it." He pulled her back into his arms. Before he could take it farther, she stepped back and looked around. He was right. No one was in sight and even the buildings were not visible from there. Kneeling on the ground, she unzipped his pants and pulled his briefs down slightly. His cock bounced readily out of his pants and was already hard. Using her tongue, she licked around the head to tease him. In anticipation, his cock shuddered. Unwilling to wait any longer, he grabbed the back of her hair and pushed himself entirely into her mouth.

John leaned his head back and took in the pleasurable sensations that were flooding through his body. Although this was good, it was not enough. He needed more. Sitting on the ground, he pulled her on top of him and lifted her skirt up.

"But John, what if someone comes?" she protested laughingly. By the way she said it, John knew that she did not mean it at all.

"Don't worry, we will hear them. Besides, you're in a skirt. It is not that hard to put your clothes on." He kissed down the side of her neck as he waited for her to respond. Her response was almost instantaneous. Slipping off her lace panties, she slid herself down on his cock. Tricia closed her eyes and moaned as the intense pleasure overwhelmed her body. At this moment, she did not care who walked by or saw them. She just knew that she wanted him more than she had ever wanted anybody in her life. Rocking her hips back and forth gently at first, she was unable to contain her desire. She pressed her hands into his chest so tightly for traction that her fingernails scratched his skin. Moving faster and faster, she took the entirety of him inside her body.

Noises were heard in the distance. John shook his head. His face was flushed with exertion as he grabbed her hips to keep him on top of her. "Don't leave. Not yet," he said. He pulled her hips forcefully against her as they began to orgasm together. An intense, bright ecstasy passed through her mind as she orgasmed. The noises were approaching closer to the hidden spot they were at. Pulling herself off him instantly, she pulled her clothes back on while he buttoned his pants. Brushing her hair back, she just finished readjusting herself when Stuart walked by.

"Hey! Here you are, John. I was looking all over for you. Some of the guests have started to arrive and you need to be there to welcome them." Stuart's eyes took in the scene in front of him. Although their flushed faces showed that something could have transpired, Stuart respected both of them enough not to say anything.

John nodded. "I will be there shortly. I am just figuring out Tricia's position over the next few weeks." Stuart returned to the church. As soon as he was out of sight, John turned to Tricia. "Tricia... Tricia..." he leaned and kissed her passionately. "Stay with me, Tricia. I know we both feel guilty, but this keeps happening for a reason. We were meant to be together." He kissed her again. For a moment, Tricia let herself become lost in the thought of his fantasy. Then the real world set in around her.

"But John... What would your friends think? And the servants? They will figure out at some point that this started before her death. Do you want people thinking that about you? Plus, there's a chance that you just bonded with me because of the stress of your wife's death. What if your feelings change?"

John shook his head. "Screw everybody else, I don't care. And my feelings are real. From the moment I saw you at the hospital, I felt an instant attraction. I was afraid from that moment on that I would be unfaithful. If Rebecca had not been so certain that you were the right nurse, I would never have assented to having such a temptation around me daily."

Closing her eyes, Tricia let him run his hands along her tan arms. "I will consider it, but I cannot make a guarantee. Let me think about staying for a while. I still want to make sure that we are both doing the right thing." She turned to walk back to the church. Noticing that the room was full, she chose a seat by the other servants and waited for everyone to arrive. As John entered the church, their eyes met for a moment and a flash of passion shot between them that had an almost tangible quality. Noticing this look, Stuart remained silent again. It was not his place to question and he honestly did not see too much harm in it. Unlike many of the other servants, he had seen the toll the last few years took on John whenever John came to the kitchen for late night snacks. A little happiness would do him good.

Chapter Six

Sitting at home later, Tricia was startled when the phone rang. To her surprise, it was her brother, Tyrone, on the phone. She could hear him crying on the other end of the line. "Tyrone, what's wrong?" her voice was concerned. With all of the work in the last few months, she had forgotten to call him or her mother for at least a few weeks.

Tyrone gained control of his voice. "I need you back here, Tricia. I don't know what to do. Mom is sick, Tricia."

Tricia leaned back in the chair as all of the energy left her body. She could not handle this. "What's wrong?"

"It started with her forgetting small things a few years ago. I brushed it off, but apparently she was hiding how bad her memory was really getting. Yesterday, the cops called because they found her wandering the streets. She had completely forgotten where she was or where she was going." Tyrone paused.

"Alzheimer's?" she asked.

"Yes. I asked her what was wrong and she wouldn't or couldn't tell me. So I searched her house and found an unpaid doctor's receipt. We went in earlier today and

I made her let me in for the appointment. He said that she is in the late stages of Alzheimer's and she also suffers from cardiovascular disease." Tyrone took a breath. "Tricia, I'm worried. If she has heart problems, she needs to take medication. There is no way that she is remembering to even eat healthfully. I doubt that she takes her medicine."

Tricia closed her eyes in pain. It had been more than a year since her last visit, and she had spent most of that visit with friends or other family members. As a nurse, she should have noticed. "Are you able to stay with her?"

Tyrone's voice became even more worried. "No, I can't. I can take a few days off of work, but I can't be here for her all the time. Could you come home? I hate to ask you this, but I can't do it and you are the best nurse I know."

"Yes, I can." She replied.

They talked for a few more minutes on the phone before hanging up. Tricia sighed. This decided it. There would be no way that she could stay with John now. She had to be there for her mother and brother.

Getting in the car, she drove back to John's mansion. Surprised guards let her inside and she made her way up to the office. Even though it was just a few hours after the funeral, she knew that John would be there. He probably wouldn't be working, but the office was his favorite place to unwind.

Entering the room, Tricia was immediately embraced by John. "Have you decided, my love? Will you stay here with me? I thought it would take longer, but I am so glad to see you." His face looked genuinely excited.

Resting her head on his chest, she replied. "No, John, I can't. My brother just told me that my mother is sick. I need to take care of her now."

John stepped back. His face was crestfallen and even his shoulders drooped in disappointment. "Do you really have to? If you don't want to stay, you could just tell me."

Tricia shook her head. "You can visit if you want to. She really is sick and my brother can't stay all day with her. I do want to stay with you, but this makes the choice easy. I must take care of my mother."

Pulling her into him, John held his hand against her neck as he kissed her. Her hair still gave off the intoxicating scent of jasmine that he loved. "Tricia, I understand." His face was pained and his voice sounded strained. "I understand that you need to do this. But also... please know that you can come back. If your mother improves or if you find someone else to care for her, you can return and be with me."

Tricia kissed him gently on the lips and looked into his soft brown eyes. "I cannot promise anything, but I will try if I can. As long as I am able to though, I will take care of my mother. I want to take care of her." Kissing him again, she turned toward the door. "Goodbye, John," she whispered wistfully as she left the office.

-To be continued in Book 2-

Book Two

Chapter One

TRICIA SAT in her childhood home and gazed at the wall; today had been particularly trying. In addition to flying from Seattle to Dallas, she had immediately started to take care of her mother. Diagnosed with Alzheimer's, her mother also had a heart condition, and like always, had refused to take any medicine. Before she had moved to Texas, her mother had lived in Alabama where she saw the effects of the Tuskegee Experiment that lasted long after the experiment had officially ended. African-American men who were diagnosed with syphilis in the 1930s were tracked for forty years to see the long-term effects of the disease. Even when a cure came out in the 1950s, the doctors had not cured the men. Instead, they told patients who wanted to be treated that they had already been given medicine. Hundreds and thousands of people from the families were infected and affected by the trial.

Due to this, Tricia's mother refused to listen to white doctors. The crotchety old woman refused to believe that medicine would help or that anything was wrong with her. After an hour of trying and failing to convince her mother to take the medicine, Tricia had finally given up. She had made some bread pudding with dinner and sprinkled crumbled tablets into her mother's portions. It may not have been the most honest solution, but it worked. Now, Tricia was just exhausted.

Moving back to the kitchen, she started to make herself a cup of chamomile tea. With her mother in bed, it was time to drink some tea and unwind. Thankfully, she only had another two days until the weekend. Her brother Tyrone had promised to take care of her mother over the weekend so that Tricia could take a break and catch up with some old friends.

Sipping her cup of tea, she went to the bathroom and turned on the bathwater. As bubbles and warm water filled the tub, she slowly began to remove her clothes. Only a few days ago, she had left John. After telling him of her decision to return home to her mother, she had not talked to him or seen him again. Their brief fling had been as passionate as it was short-lived. She had taken care of his wife during the final stages of ALS. Although they had tried to stop their sexual desires from taking over, John and Tricia had made love more than a couple of times. It was wrong and she still felt guilty. Despite her ethical concerns, she found herself wishing that she was still with him. His confident nature and unwavering conscience had attracted her to him from the moment they met.

Easing herself into the water, Tricia laughed to herself. If only her mother knew that she had slept with a rich, white man. She would never forgive her. Tricia picked up Jane Eyre and tried to read, but even her favorite novel could not distract her mind. She wanted John more than anything. It was impossible for her to go without sex anymore. After realizing how fulfilling and satisfying sex could be with him, she was not willing to go back to her normal celibate lifestyle. She glanced at the bathroom door and saw that it was locked. Moving her hand down her body, she closed her eyes and pretended that her hand was John's. Tricia ran her fingertips around the dark cocoa-colored skin around her nipples and then drew it down further. Initially, she started playing with the soft lips around her clit. This was not enough to satisfy her for long. She moved her clit in slow circles as she imagined John entering her for the first time in the office. The sex had been so magnetic, so electrically charged. She imagined his hard muscles moving against her and moaned.

The moan startled her. She looked at the door to see if her mother had heard anything. There were no sounds from the rest of the house. Moving her hand down along her body again, she moved her fingers faster and faster. Tricia could feel herself approaching orgasm when a sudden sound surprised her. The shrill ringing of the phone pierced the air. For a moment, Tricia thought about ignoring it and finishing herself off. With a belabored sigh, she stood up and grabbed a towel. It could be someone important for her mother.

Exiting the bathroom, she rushed to reach the phone before it stopped ringing. "Hello?" she said with a breathy voice. Holding the phone away from her mouth, she took a deep breath to slow her heart rate down.

The voice on the other end was high-pitched and ecstatic. "Tricia! I can't believe that you are finally home!"

"Oh," Tricia cursed herself. It was just her best friend, Tenaya. They had grown up and gone to school together. Although she was glad to hear from her, she also wished that she had just ignored the phone and called back later. She tried to make her voice sound happier than she was. "Hey, Tenaya. How is everything?"

"Everything is just great. I started working for a new school and really love the other teachers. Your brother told me that you were back, but I just could not believe it. How could you not call me the moment that you returned home?" Tenaya's voice had a teasing quality to it that made Tricia smile.

"I am so sorry. I was going to call immediately, but spent the first few hours trying to convince my mom that she should take her medication."

"She still thinks that the white doctor is lying to her?" Tenaya laughed. Some things never changed.

Tricia rolled her eyes. "You know how she is," she paused. "So what's new with you?"

For the next 20 minutes, Tricia caught up with Tenaya on the phone. Finally it was decided that she would come over on Saturday night for dinner and a romantic comedy marathon. Hanging up the phone, Tricia heaved a sigh of relief. At least one part of her life was going well.

Chapter Two

Tricia tossed the bottle of pills to Tyrone. "Remember," she said. "You need to crumble this up in her food. She will not touch it otherwise. Oh, and make sure she actually eats all of her food. She has developed a bad habit of feeding some of her food to the dog. And..." she looked around as if trying to think of the last thing to tell him.

Tyrone held up his hand to stop her from continuing. "Look, I got it. I can handle this. Just go enjoy yourself. You work hard enough. I don't want to see you back until the wee hours of the morning." He hugged her. "Be safe, little sister."

Smiling, Tricia picked up her purse and left the house. She was finally getting to have some fun. When she was working for John and Rebecca, she had spent most of her evenings sitting at home. With her busy work schedule, she had never really had time to make friends. Maybe returning home was a good thing after all.

Knocking on the door, Tricia nearly fell over as Tenaya tackled her with a bear hug. "I can't believe that you are finally here!" she exclaimed. "Tell me everything, girl!"

Walking inside the house, Tricia started to speak and stopped mid-sentence. Standing before her was the towering figure of Rod. As Tenaya's older brother, Rod had grudgingly let them tag along to the movies and shopping mall. Tricia had had a crush on him as a girl, but was never more to him than his little sister's friend. When she left to go to nursing school, Rod was already studying in college. Apparently, he had grown up well. His buttoned up shirt fit tightly across his bulging chest muscles and he was at least six inches taller than in high school.

Tenaya glanced over at Tricia. "Oh, I forgot to ask. Is it all right if Rod has dinner with us? I figured you may want to spend some time catching up with him as well."

Tricia nodded, unable to speak. Rod smiled. "How are you doing, Tricia? You aren't a little girl in pigtails anymore, I see."

Regaining her ability to speak, Tricia laughed. "And you have grown up a bit, too. How are you doing?"

Rod shrugged. "Fairly good. After college, I decided to get my real estate license. I've been working on some projects to help gentrify the neighborhood."

Her eyes brightened. "I was wondering what was going on. A lot of the stores seem to be coming back."

He nodded. "It takes time, but slowly things will change. Just gotta keep hoping and working toward the goal."

Smiling, Tenaya put her arm around Tricia and brought her toward the kitchen. Calling over the shoulder for Rod to check the mail, she whispered in Tricia's ear. "What was that with you guys? Do you like him?"

Tricia blushed. Had she been that obvious in checking him out? She shook her head.

Giggling, Tenaya wagged her finger at Tricia. "I know when you are crushing on someone. Here, I'll talk to him after you leave and see about getting you a date."

"No, you do not need to do that. He probably doesn't even notice me." Tricia tried to convince Tenaya that she did not need her help in getting a date, but nothing she said changed her mind. Sitting down at the table, Tenaya spooned out some collard greens, baked beans, corn bread and ham.

"Did you miss eating southern food up in Seattle? What do they eat there anyway? Tree bark and granola?" Tenaya laughed good-naturedly.

Rolling her eyes, Tricia took some more corn bread. "No, they do not eat tree bark, although there was a lot of granola in the stores. I don't know. I guess I just ate whatever the chef made."

Rod's eyebrows shot up as he walked into the kitchen and sat down at the table. "A chef? How did you get your own chef?"

Tricia had both siblings looking at her now. "Well, it was not my chef. John and Rebecca had a chef and servants to run the house."

"Huh," Tenaya said. "So you lived pretty well. What made you leave? With the money you made, you could have just hired a nurse."

Tricia shook her head. "No, I needed to be here for my mom."

"But Tyrone is here. Did you just hate the boss? Was he mean?"

Blushing slightly, Tricia focused on eating a bite of baked beans. She did not want to talk about John. Tenaya knew her well enough to figure out what had gone on between them. "No, it was fine," she said. Glancing up, she motioned over to Tenaya. "How's teaching going?"

Tenaya rolled her eyes. She knew that Tricia was changing the subject, but did not want to press the matter with Rod here. "It is going pretty well. Since it is the start of the school year, I have been just trying to put the fear of God into my students. So far, it seems to be working. They have not been acting up too much and seem to actually be doing pretty well with the latest book report."

Before long, dinner was over. Rod stood up to clear the table. "As soon as I wash these dishes for you, I will head out. I got a meeting with a client and I suspect that you ladies need some girl time." Turning to the sink, he began to wash the dishes. After thanking him, Tricia and Tenaya went to the living room.

Plopping down on the couch, Tenaya looked over at Tricia. "So tell me."

Tricia was taken back. She had hoped Tenaya did not notice her blushing earlier. "Tell you what?"

"You know," Tenaya needled her in the ribs. "What was with your bosses? Did they beat you? Forget to pay? Harass you? You were avoiding the subject during dinner."

Shrugging her shoulders, Tricia tried not to say anything. Another sharp look from Tenaya told her that it would not be that easy to change the subject this time. "Fine, Fine. You win. I slept with him."

Tenaya squealed. "Oh my god! You did what? With the billionaire? The guy with his own chef?" Her grip on one of the couch's pillows tightened with excitement. "Oh! Tell me! How was it?"

Tricia smiled. If she was going to share her secret with anyone, it might as well be Tenaya. "It was... amazing. But more than just the sex, there was this feeling that it could have become something more."

Frowning, Tenaya thought for a moment. "But why would you ever leave then? If you thought it could be love someday, why didn't you try to make it work?"

Tricia shook her head. "I can't. What would everyone think? What would I think? The poor black girl from the 'hood dating the billionaire? At best, they would think that he was taking advantage of me. At worst, everyone would say that I am a gold digger. Not to mention, could you imagine the reaction? He may be just a businessman, but John's money has attracted the tabloid more than once in the past. If he was with a black girl, every newspaper in the country would pick up that story. The country is getting more liberal, but there are still people who are against an interracial couple."

Tenaya laughed. "Like your mother, for one. But really, what if he was the one? Couldn't you have at least tried staying with him just to see? You could have just let your true love go."

Shaking her head, Tricia patted Tenaya on the hand. "You are a hopeless romantic. This is not one of your romantic comedies; it is my life. If I screw up, I cannot just push rewind. Do you really think that there is just one true love for each person?"

Tenaya nodded her head with conviction. "Yes, I do."

"Well, when you find your true love, I will try dating John. Until then, let me live my own private life. Besides, you were trying to hook me up with your brother just twenty minutes ago." Tricia laughed. "You are truly incorrigible. Here, pick out a movie and I will make us some popcorn." Realizing that the topic was over, Tenaya settled in for a long night of romantic movies.

Arriving home around midnight, Tricia slid her key in the lock. As she walked into the entryway, she caught sight of some flowers on the table with a card. Confused, she opened the envelope. Inside was a note from Rod with his number. Along with his number, the message read, "Call me tomorrow if you are interested in going on a date tomorrow night. Dress up and we will take the town by storm." Smiling, she put the card back

in the envelope. She would call him in the morning. It
would be good for her to see someone other than John.

Chapter Three

Stepping out of the shower, Tricia slipped into a black thong and garters. Fastening a matching bra, she stepped into a bright red dress. The vivid red color contrasted perfectly with her dark skin. As she applied makeup, she realized that she was actually getting nervous. Initially, she had not worried too much about the date. Still wrapped up in John, she had figured that this date would just serve as a welcome distraction. But as the date approached, she found herself becoming increasingly nervous.

The sound of the doorbell disrupted her musings. He was early. Thankfully, she had started getting ready far sooner than she needed to. Spraying on some perfume, she slipped into red heels and went to answer the door. In front of her, Rod was dressed in a black suit and tie. She raised an eyebrow. "Exactly how dressed up should I be?" she asked.

Rod smiled and she felt herself grow weak in her knees. He was so terribly attractive. He shook his head. "What you are wearing is perfect. You look unbelievably stunning."

Walking her to the car, he opened her door. Unable to think of anything to say, she just thanked him and he started the car. "So... where are we going?" she asked.

"I have a reservation at the Five Sixty restaurant in Reunion Tower," he said. She raised her eyebrows. Reunion Tower was an iconic part of the Dallas skyline. It was essentially a giant ball that rotated at the top of a building. From the restaurant, people could see the whole city while they ate. Getting a reservation would have been difficult and exceptionally expensive.

"I am guessing that the real estate business is going well," she said.

In response, Rod laughed. "I suppose it is. Honestly, I just figured you deserved a treat after the last few weeks. Tenaya told me that the patient you were taking care of ended up dying recently. I can't imagine that this past month has been easy for you at all."

Tricia shook her head. If only he knew. "No, it really has not been a good month." She paused. If Tenaya told him about Rebecca's death, what else could she have said? "So, what else did Tenaya tell you?" she asked Rod.

Shrugging, Rod patted her hand reassuringly. "Not too much. I tried pumping her for information, but she said I should get to know you on my own instead of cheating."

"Sounds like her," Tricia laughingly responded in relief. She was not ready to talk about John with Rod. Honestly, she may never tell him about John. There was no reason for him to become jealous or worry about another guy, especially at this point in the relationship.

After finally locating a parking spot and getting into the building, Tricia and Rod waited to be shown to their table. As they walked across the restaurant, Tricia gasped in surprise. "It is so beautiful!"

Rod glanced over at her. "Wait, have you never been here?"

"Never. I always wanted to go, but it seemed like such a waste of money when I was a student. After I graduated, there was just never time on my visits to Mom."

Smiling, Rod slid his arm around her waist and pulled her close. "Well, I am glad that I get to be your first then. The food is actually as good as the view, so I think you are going to have an excellent time."

Sitting at the table, Tricia let Rod order for her. Half the menu items were written in completely unintelligible French. While he ordered, Tricia relaxed and let the French phrases roll over her. After the waiter left, she looked over at Rod. "So tell me, how do you know how to order here? It isn't really a talent that you would learn in the old neighborhood."

Lifting his glass to her, Rod took a sip of wine. "True, but there are always other ways. I studied in France during college. My time there was fortunate because I often take out-of-town investors here to go over bids and potential projects."

Tricia smiled. "You are a truly interesting person. If I get to know you better, will I continue to uncover new layers to your personality?"

Rod shrugged. "I suppose so, but I really think that is true for everyone." He started to say more, but the first course had arrived. Falling silent for a moment, the pair waited for the waiter to leave before resuming their conversation. Tricia was surprised. Unlike most first dates, spending time with Rod felt so natural. She felt completely comfortable around him and the conversation flowed through dinner. By the time the check came, she found herself unusually sad. This wonderful evening was about to come to an end.

Standing up from the table, Tricia let Rod hold her around the waist again as they left. It felt so different being with him. Unlike John, she did not have to hide their blossoming relationship or worry about the reaction of other people. Anyone in the restaurant would just see an attractive black couple if they looked over.

Arriving at the car, Tricia hesitated for a moment. "What is it?" Rod asked.

She shook her head. "I am not sure. I just realized that I really do not want this evening to be over." Beyond enjoying the evening, she found herself wanting to bring him home with her. She had never managed to reach orgasm the other day and really needed to have sex.

Rod smiled widely. "Well, we can always go somewhere else. Where do you want to go?"

Perhaps it was the wine or perhaps she was far more confident than she thought. No matter what the reason was, she was as surprised as Rod by the next sentence that came out of her mouth. "What if we check into a hotel?"

Stunned, Rod did not say anything for a moment. Tricia blushed deeply and shook her head. "Sorry, forget I said that."

Shaking his head, Rod slammed the door of the car and pushed her against it. Pressing his body against hers, he tilted her head up to his and kissed her. The kiss was long and passionate. Pulling away, he kept his eyes locked on hers. She could feel his pulse beating fast against hers. Rod kissed her again. "Yes, we can do that. I was just surprised. I would love to find a hotel."

Getting in the car, he held her hand in his. Now that she had asked him to go to a hotel, he did not know what to say. Throughout the evening, Rod had fantasized about sleeping with her. He had imagined how her breasts would look and what her legs would feel like wrapped around his. Now that this was actually happening, he was dumbfounded. In the seat next to him, Tricia was silent as well. She could not believe that she had been so forward, but she also did not regret it. She wanted this to happen.

Checking into the hotel, Tricia and Rod walked hand in hand up the stairs. Between them was an unspoken agreement not to talk about what was about to happen. It seemed as even a word that suggested the coming pleasure would break the spell. Self-conscious and restrained, Rod unlocked the door and stepped back to let Tricia through.

The door shut and Tricia was left staring at Rod. Neither of them was able to make a move. Before Rod, was a vision in red that could be all his in an instant. The thrill of the coming sexual encounter overwhelmed him. He pulled out a pocket knife. Tricia raised an eyebrow. "What is that for?"

He looked down at the knife and seemed almost surprised to see it. "I want... I want to cut your dress off of you and see your breasts pop out and expose the entirety of your body." Rod fell silent as he finished talking. Some type of strange desire was taking control of him and he had no clue what he was doing. It was like an entirely different person existed within him who had taken control.

Tricia nodded. Demurely, she lay back on the bed. Her long chocolate legs stretched endlessly toward Rod. Groaning with pent-up desire, he stepped toward her. Grasping the top of her dress in his hand, he ripped straight down the middle with his pocket knife. As the sides of the dress fell, her breasts bounced pleasingly out. Perfectly round and well-shaped, her nipples were hard enough to see through her bra. Rod lifted her legs and pushed her back farther on the bed. Reaching between her legs, he felt her cunt and realized how wet she was. At the moment he touched her, Tricia moaned. She had been waiting for this for days. Tricia no longer cared about her reputation or about what Rod may think of her. If he was not inside of her soon, she would explode.

Rocking her hips upward, she felt his fingers go in her. Swirling around inside of her body, she immediately realized that this was not enough. All it did was tease her and make her want him more. Tricia sat up and wrapped her legs around his lower body.

Reaching her hands up, she clasped his neck and pulled him down. "I need you," she whispered. The sound of her sultry, soft voice drove him to madness. Pulling off his pants in a clean motion, he entered her immediately. There was no time to get a condom, ask about birth control or see if she wanted sex. He had to have her now. Pressing her wrists into the bed, he thrust as hard as he could into her. The pain brought tears to her eyes, but she enjoyed it. She wanted it rough and wanted to feel the full force of him inside her. Arching her back, she brought her hips up against his. This sexualized motion brought him close to orgasm instantly. Gasping, he grabbed her hips with his hands.

"Not yet," he said. "You do not get to have your way yet." Leaning back on his heels, he brought her onto his lap without pulling out of her. With her weight above him, gravity caused him to enter even deeper inside her. The supreme pleasure caused her to cry out.

"Don't," she cried, "Don't stop." Tricia tried to move her hips against his, but he held her body tightly. Like a wild animal, she worked on moving against his body. Again and again, he rebutted her advances. Tricia's rising sexual frustration turned him on and he wanted to make her wait. Finally, he released her. Shoving him back down onto the bed, she put her hands behind her on his knees. Arching backwards, she managed to get the entire length of his cock into her body. Gasping in pleasure, she moved her hips hard against his. All of her inhibitions had left her entirely and she cried out in pleasure as she felt her orgasm approaching. As the bright ecstasy of orgasm passed through her body, a brief glimpse of Rod's face told her that he was orgasming as well. Sweaty and flushed, the pair fell back on the bed.

She rolled over to look at him. "That was amazing. Do you want...?"

Rod smiled. "Again? Of course." He grabbed his tie from the ground. "Tie me to the chair first. I like it when you take control." He kissed the inside of her wrist gently. "It is unbelievably sexy." Moving to the chair, he waited patiently for her to come to him. This was going to be a long, but pleasurable, night.

Moving over to the chair, Tricia smiled wickedly. Her eyes gleamed brightly in the dim light. Kneeling behind the chair, she tied his body tightly. His hands were unable to move at all.

Returning to the bed, she searched the covers for Rod's pocket knife. Finding it, she went back to Rod. She flicked out the blade and ran it against his skin. Tracing his nipple with the tip of the blade, she cut a hair off by accident.

Leaning close to him, she whispered in his ear. "Too close?" she asked.

He shook his head. "Use me as you wish."

Tricia ran the knife down his body and allowed it to gently press against his cock. The sudden attention caused him to harden. As he became hard, his cock came closer to the motionless knife. Groaning in agony, he tried to think of anything that would make him less turned on. Smiling, Tricia pulled the knife away. The instant it was gone, his cock jerked back to attention. Trembling with anticipation, Rod moaned. "Please, please, don't keep teasing me like this."

Tricia smiled. "If you think you want me now, just wait." Sitting down on the bed, she spread her legs and started to touch herself. From across the room, Rod struggled to get a clear view. Each time he tried to look, the soft pink folds of her lips were out of sight. Minutes passed in agonizing succession as he waited for her to stop teasing him so badly. Finally, she came over to him on the chair. Straddling her body across his, she sank down without warning on his cock. The slick wetness welcomed him deep inside her and the sudden pleasure brought him close to orgasm. Gasping, he tried to move away. "I can't. You have teased me for too long. I won't be able to hold back."

Grinning, Tricia leaned down to bite his nipple. Straightening her body again, she moved her hips violently against his. The motion set his entire body trembling as he struggled to control himself. "You better hold back or I will whip you later."

The thought of her running a whip along his body was too much. Precum seeped from him as he used every mental technique possible to hold back. Tricia did not help it. Seduced by the power, she wanted to watch his agony as he tried not to orgasm. Moving her hips rhythmically, she lifted them with each repetition so his cock was fully removed before it entered her again. As she sought to tease him further, a surprise feeling started to blossom within her. She was close to orgasm as well. Unable to tease any longer, her control completely weakened. She found herself thrusting her body against his in wanton abandon. As he slid into her, each nerve ending in her body was set on fire with a passion so intense it clouded her entire mind. Conscious thoughts left her and she threw herself into him. Harder and harder she forced her cunt against him until he broke.

Throbbing and jerking madly, he came inside of her and filled her completely. The throbbing of his cock struck some deep, evolutionary force within her and she came. Her muscles and tendons convulsed throughout her entire body. The strength of her orgasm caused her leg to cramp, but she could not stop moving against him. The pleasure was too intense and unreal for her to ever want to stop. Finally, the sensation became too overpowering. As her orgasm ended, she pulled her body off of his and reluctantly untied him. Even the simple act of unfastening his bonds reminded her again of what she wanted. Rod was in for an even longer night.

Chapter Four

Several months passed quickly in succession. The romance with Rod was quickly picking up speed. In addition to mind-blowing sex, Tricia was quickly discovering the many facets of his personality. On weekends, Rod coached a basketball team at the youth center and he secretly enjoyed gardening. Every day, it seemed like Tricia was learning new things about him. She could not believe how lucky she was to finally find someone who was just right for her. Her relationship with Rod was not the only good luck she had. Recently, Tyrone had moved back into their mother's house. This meant that Tricia could have more evenings off. At first, she had avoided telling Tyrone about Rod because she did not know where the relationship was going. He figured out on his own a few weeks previously and Tricia found herself not caring. At last, she was in a healthy relationship.

Humming as she went into the bedroom, Tricia set down the breakfast tray. Reaching over, she shook her mother's arm. How strange. Normally, her mother would wake up as soon as the sun was up. Her mother did not respond. Shaking her arm again, Tricia was met with no reaction. Horrified, she took her pulse. She could not feel anything. Reaching for the phone, she dialed 911 with a shaky hand. Telling the operator her address, she told them to come quick. Her mother may be dead.

As she waited for the ambulance, Tricia sank down to the ground. Her mother had been doing better. Her Alzheimer's was not improving, but it also was not getting worse. She had even been taking her heart medication willingly. Unless... Tricia frowned and rushed to look in her mother's dresser drawer. Tossing the clothes out, she finally found what she had been searching for. A small jewelry box in her mother's dresser was full of pills. She had been slipping them out of her mouth when Tricia was not looking.

Stepping back in horror, Tricia fell against the wall again. Sliding down into a squatting position, she hung her head in her hands. Sobs racked her body. She had known that her mother was sick, but death had always seemed like a faraway, unreal outcome.

A knock was heard and Tricia stood up to let the paramedics in. People and a flurry of equipment passed around her. As the paramedics tested her mother's pulse and checked for any signs of breathing, the room became increasingly gloomy. It did not seem like her mother was ever going to come back from this. Finally, the dreaded moment came when one of the paramedics looked up and shook his head. "I'm sorry," was all that he said.

Tricia ran out of the room. She could not be there. The entire world seemed to be closing in around her and suffocating her. She had to go somewhere or do something. If she went to sleep, maybe she would wake up and realize that this was a dream.

Leaving the house, she shuffled along. For once, the fall rain was just a light drizzle instead of a downpour. As she thought disconnectedly about this one bright side, she heard a crash of thunder. Texas's normal torrential rain started up and she was drenched in moments. As normal people sought cover or pulled out umbrellas, Tricia kept walking. The rain matched her mood. In the coldness and the stinging rain, she found the same physical sensations that she was feeling within her. A cold emptiness filled her soul and made it impossible for her to think. This year had been filled with too much stress and too much death. She needed out.

Back at the house, Tyrone had arrived home to discover the paramedics taking his mother to a funeral home. Sinking down into the couch, he waited while they relayed what had happened with his sister. Despite his pain, Tyrone managed to think about his sister. She needed help. Calling up Rod, he explained the situation in as few words as he could. As soon as Rod heard what the problem was, he immediately told Tyrone that he would find her and make everything right again. Hitting the streets in his car, he drove up and down each road in search of her. Some of the low-lying streets had already started to flood, but Rod drove straight through them.

Rounding the corner, Rod caught sight of her shivering under an awning. Pulling up the car, he jumped out and pulled off his jacket. Wrapping it around her, he brought Tricia to the car and sat her down. She was completely senseless. As he started to drive, he kept glancing over at her with worry in his eyes. Tricia was completely falling apart. Rod drove to her house and packed a bag for her as she sat motionless on the couch. Calling the office, he told them that he was going to take a few days off. He needed to take her somewhere away from the grief and let her recover.

Getting back in the car, he drove silently to the town of Muenster. An hour away from Dallas, the German village was a completely different setting and may help her recover from her sudden shock. As soon as he checked into the hotel room, Tricia fell onto the bed and passed out.

For several days, Rod stayed with her in the room. With brief breaks for crying, Tricia spent the entire time sleeping. Finally one morning, she woke up and sat up in the bed. Her eyes seemed clearer than they had been for days.

Looking up from his book, Rod smiled gently. "Are you okay now?" he asked. His voice had a soft note of concern.

Tricia stretched wearily. "How long have I been out?"

Rod stepped over to the bed and sat down next to her. "You have been asleep or catatonic for about two days. I thought a change of pace could help you feel better. Did I do the right thing?"

Tricia stood up and looked out the window. Bewildered, she turned around. "Where in the world did you take me?" The Bavarian-style houses were completely foreign to her.

Laughing, Rod stepped behind her and wrapped his arms around her shoulders. "You're still in Texas, my dear. We're just in Muenster."

Tricia turned. The enormity of what he had done for her came crashing down. "So you waited with me for two days? Why? You did not have to do that. My brother would have taken care of me."

Rod kissed the back of her head. "Your brother could have, but I wanted to. I love you, Tricia."

She turned to look at him and was unable to think of anything to say. He had never told her that he loved her before. "You love me?"

Rod nodded. "I was going to make some grand romantic gesture and then tell you, but now seemed like the right time." He held her closer. Gradually, he realized that she had not said anything in return. "Wait, you never responded. Do you…" he paused and tried again. "Do you love me, too?"

Tricia did not know what to say. She did not know if she loved him. Honestly, she had put off the thought of a future relationship. She had enjoyed living in the present and taking each date as it arrived. Turning to face him, she ran her hand along his face gently. "I don't really know right now. There is far too much for me to take in. I need to deal with the loss of my mother before I can really think about anything else. When I do say that I love you, you will be able to know that I mean it though."

Rod tried to hide his disappointment and turned to start packing. "It's okay, Tricia. You are right. I should not have sprung this on you. Don't worry about it for now. I just want to help you get through this."

Picking up the suitcases, Rod left the hotel room to put them in the car. From the window, Tricia watched him walk across the parking lot. Was she so heartless for not loving him? She really did not know how she felt about anything right now. Sighing, she walked into the bathroom and managed to find a complimentary toothbrush. By the time Rod returned, she had showered and brushed her teeth. She was finally starting to feel a lot more normal.

The ride home was completely silent. Neither partner could think of anything to say that did not involve their relationship or feelings for each other. After a ride that seemed like it stretched on for years, Rod finally pulled in front of Tricia's house. Helping her out of the car, he wheeled her suitcase to the door for her. Kissing her gently on the forehead, he returned to the car and left Tricia to face the house on her own. For several moments, she stood silently in front of the closed door. If she went inside, she would have to face a house that no longer held her mother. She would have to start packing her mother's things and look into preparing for the funeral. Even worse, she would have to face a stream of questions from her brother about how she was doing.

Sighing deeply, she finally pushed the key into the lock. Stepping into the entryway, she fumbled for the light switch in the dark. As the light flipped on, she caught sight of some roses on the entryway table. Frowning slightly, she let out a sigh of exasperation. Rod just could not leave it alone. Adding flowers to his sudden confession of love was too much. The extra attention only served to cause more stress for her.

Reaching for the flowers, she brought them into the kitchen to throw them away. At the last moment, she decided to open the card. He deserved to at least have the card read. Slipping the card out, her jaw dropped.

The flowers were not from Rod. They were from John. In his block writing, he had scrawled out a happy birthday note to her. Tricia smiled wanly. She had completely forgotten that her birthday was today. Her brother must have accepted these flowers for her.

Sitting down at the kitchen table, she scrutinized the note. It said that John would be in town next week. He would be dealing with business, but wanted to meet her for business if she was available. On the note, he had left a number for her to call.

Pressing the note to her chest, Tricia shut her eyes. What was she supposed to do? She had not thought about John for weeks. Every time she had sex with Rod, her feelings for John had slowly started to dissipate. Now, he had shoved his way back into her life. She did not know what to do. With Rod, the sex was amazing and the relationship made sense. John would never be an easy person to have a relationship with, but she connected with him on a totally different level.

Leaning back in the chair, Tricia realized she had another problem. Rod was Tenaya's brother. If she hurt Rod, Tenaya would never forgive her. Ironically, seeing John may not even matter. By not loving him fully, she had already hurt him. For several long minutes, she sat indecisively. She wanted to see John so badly, but it went against everything that she felt was right. Impulsively, she reached for the phone and dialed. She did not care what was right. She wanted to see John again.

-To be continued in Book 3-

Book Three

Chapter One

TRICIA WAITED impatiently at the door. Her hands were shaking with nervous tension. It had taken an unbelievable amount of time to do her makeup because her hands kept jerking as she tried to apply lipstick and mascara. Finally, it seemed like it was almost time for John to arrive. Trying to calm her nerves, she sat down on the couch.

Although it seemed like forever ago, Tricia had once been in love with John. Despite their better intentions, they had succumbed to an animalistic desire and had sex—more times than she could count. Tricia had been nursing his sick wife, Rebecca, until she died. After Rebecca's death, Tricia had returned home and taken care of her mother. Now, it seemed like anything was possible. After burying her mother, John had sent her a message and flowers for her birthday. She was going to have dinner with him tonight.

Tricia smoothed her dress awkwardly. She had worn this red dress not long before she had finally had sex with John for the first time. Although she had pretended not to notice, she had seen him watching her slim curves move and strain against the fabric. She cursed herself silently. How could she possibly be trying to dress up for him? Since Tricia had returned home, she had dated Rod. Attractive and successful, Rod was a wealthy real estate developer. More importantly, he was kind, funny and actually black. Although times were changing, dating someone of the same race would still make her life easier. Ruining things with Rod would be terrible. He was her best friend, Tenaya's, brother and she would probably lose her friend as well as her boyfriend.

Standing up, Tricia walked over to the phone. She wanted to call John and tell him that she could not make it. Being around John would be an impossible temptation for her. Dialing the phone number, she waited until his voicemail picked it up. Unwilling to cancel a date with a message, she went over to the couch to sit down again. Before she could get comfortable, she heard a knock at the door.

Groaning, she managed to smile before she pulled the door open. In front of her, John stood with a handful of red roses. Smiling widely, he made a move toward her and seemed prepared to sweep her off her feet in an instant. Pushing his hand away, she gave him a hug.

Confused, John hugged her before stepping back. "You look... ravishing, Tricia. How are you?" In his voice, she could hear the unspoken question. He did not know about Rod and could not understand her hesitation.

"I'm good, John. For a while, I was confused and depressed after my mother's death. Fortunately, Rod was there to help me through it." As soon as she said this, she regretted it. Tricia had wanted to slip Rod's name in so that John would know she had a boyfriend. John's crestfallen expression made her instantly reconsider this decision. "Here, come in, come in. I can get you a cup of tea or something before we go. Did you want anything?"

Stepping inside, John seemed at ease finally. Tricia was surprised. With a net worth in the billions, it seemed strange that he should be so comfortable within her small, family house.

John regained his composure and smiled. "Sure, tea would be great. If you have any coffee, that would be even better. I just arrived on the jet and am a bit tired."

Tricia went into the kitchen. As she poured the coffee, she went over what he just said again. Carrying the cups back to him, she set them on the table. "Wait— you just got here? I thought you were here on business. When is your meeting?"

Smiling bashfully, John took a sip of coffee. "Well, that was a little stretch of the truth. Honestly, I just wanted to see you. I had hoped that enough time had passed to be respectful of my late wife so that you would finally date me again. Now, I see that I am a little too late for that." He smiled ruefully. "At any rate, this is a chance to catch up with you and have a good dinner."

Tricia smiled. "That sounds great. I'm sorry about Rod, I just..."

John held up his hand for her to stop talking. "No excuses needed. I completely understand." He finished the rest of his coffee in a gulp. "Did you want to go to that one restaurant downtown? I don't recall the name, but it was this delicious French place in a spinning ball."

Laughing, Tricia shook her head. "You mean Reunion Tower?" she paused. Rod had taken her to Reunion Tower the first time they had sex. She coughed. "Um, maybe not something so fancy. This is the first time I get to see you again, so maybe somewhere more relaxed."

He noticed that she was hiding something or trying to avoid going to Reunion Tower, but John was smart enough not to press the issue. "Sure, I have the perfect place. Do you have any cowgirl boots?"

Tricia shook her head. "What? Why?"

Laughing, John led her to his car. From the trunk, he pulled a pair of red boots that were exactly her size. Confused, she looked up at him. "How did you know that I would need them? Or that I would be dressed in red?"

Smiling, John kissed her on the forehead. Instinctively, Tricia leaned her head back for a kiss before she remembered that they were not together anymore. John hugged her instead. Pulling away, his eyes twinkled with amusement. "Well, I rather hoped you would wear red—you look so good in this dress. As for needing them, I figured that you would turn down the fancy restaurant. You're classy, but you're more in your element in the real world where people care about enjoying life—not gourmet cuisine. At any rate, I figured I'd be prepared." Pulling out a black pair of boots, he pulled them on as she put her red boots on. Holding open the door for her, he helped her into the car.

Throughout the ride, John refused to say where they were going. As they exited the freeway, she realized that they were headed toward Arlington, Texas. Confused, she glanced over at him. "Where in the world are we going?" she asked.

John shrugged as he turned a corner. "We'll be there in a second and you can see. For the full experience, I was thinking you could escort me to a rodeo in Mesquite tonight. I don't often have time to take in the sights and amusements of Texas. To be honest, I don't think that I have ever been here for anything other than business."

Pulling into the parking lot, John helped her out of the car. She glanced up at the sign. "Trail Dust Steakhouse?"

John smiled. "A client took me here once. I learned the hard way that this is a pretty relaxed place. They cut off my tie when I walked in the door."

Tricia glanced over at him to see if he was joking. "Seriously?"

Laughing, John held the restaurant door open for her. "You'll see, it's a great place, really. There should be some line dancing later on tonight as well."

Following the hostess, they arrived at their table and ordered some steaks. In the middle of the restaurant, a giant slide stretched from the second floor to the first. Children were happily running up the stairs and down the slide. As their drinks arrived, John motioned to the children. "You ever want one?"

Tricia nodded. "Yes, someday. I'm surprised you never had any children with Rebecca."

Shaking his head, John leaned back as the server set a steak in front of him. "No, we never had children. We always thought there would be more time."

Leaning back, Tricia sipped her drink as she gazed around the room. Many of the diners were dressed in western gear. Looking back at John, she picked up her knife to cut the steak. "You know that this is a weird conversation. Even if I were single, it would still be questionable about if we ever had kids. What type of life would a half-black, half-white child have? Where would they belong?"

John shrugged. "They'd figure it out. It isn't the 1960s anymore, you know. Plus, I live in Washington state. Things are a bit more liberal up there than here."

Tricia swallowed her bite. "True, but don't you think we'd have to care? As parents? We should give them the best chance they have at life." She laughed. "You tricked me into continuing this conversation." Pointing her knife teasingly at him, she shook her head. "We are only talking as old friends, John. Remember that."

John motioned to the dance floor. The children were being removed from the slide to make room for line dancing. "Well, old friend, care to dance? We don't even have to touch each other."

Smiling, Tricia consented and allowed him to lead her onto the dance floor. As the music started, she suddenly felt a thrill of exhilaration. It was like her body was finally coming back to life as she danced.

Nothing mattered in the world other than the rhythmical pulsing of boots on the wooden floor and the twanging beat of country music flowing through her veins.

Finally, she motioned to John that she had to stop. They had danced for long enough. John smiled at her with his bright, white smile. Putting his hand on her hip, he led her back to the table where he tossed a few 20 dollar bills to cover the cost of the meal. Although she felt she ought to tell him to take his hand off of her hip, she did not want to. It felt so perfect and right. It was like she had spent the last few months just waiting for this moment.

Returning to the car, John started to drive to the rodeo. Tricia placed her hand on his arm. "Wait, stop at a liquor store before we get there. It will be cheaper if we can sneak alcohol in."

John laughed. "Are we in high school?"

Rolling her eyes, Tricia snorted. "No, but us normal people we still have to save money."

Chuckling in amusement, John pulled into a liquor store and waited until she came out with a bottle of vodka. Slipping it between the folds of her purse, Tricia smiled. "That should do it. They don't search too hard."

After pulling into the rodeo, John went to buy tickets and they got into the arena without any issues. Before the event could start, they purchased a couple of cokes and surreptitiously poured several shots of vodka in each. Leaning back, John wrapped his arm around Tricia as they sat down. Again, she felt like she should tell him no and could not. With her head next to his body, she could smell his cologne and make out a few chest hairs sticking out of his shirt.

John winked at her as he caught her looking at his chest hair. "My eyes are up here, darling." He drawled in a fake southern accent.

Tricia laughed again. Already, the vodka was getting to her. "Your accent is terrible, by the way. That's closer to a Georgian accent than a Texan one."

Good-natured, John just shrugged. "Maybe you should teach me. Lay a little Southern charm on a poor northern boy like me." He grinned wickedly.

Pushing him away teasingly, Tricia leaned back as the rodeo started. Rodeo clowns flooded the area and bulls darted across the dirt. She had not gone to the rodeo since she was a child. Tricia had always begged her mom to take her here for one reason. Children under a certain age were allowed to chase after the younger bulls. If they could pull a ribbon off of the bull's horn, the child was given some type of prize. Tricia had never won, but this had not stopped her from begging her mom to bring her here every spring.

Blinking away a tear at the memory, Tricia started to stand up. John glanced up in curiosity. "I just needed to go to the lady's room. Maybe get us some more cokes."

John nodded and stood up. "No problem. I'll get the sodas and we can walk back together."

Entering the restroom, Tricia walked over to the mirror. With the rodeo still going on, there were very few women in the bathroom. She looked in the mirror. Staring back at her was a gorgeous, lively black woman with bright eyes. Surprised, she looked closer at her reflection. This was the best she had looked in weeks. Something was different in the reflection that gazed back at her. There was more life and happiness in her expression. Pausing, she pulled a lipstick out of her purse. She was going to be in so much trouble if she stayed with him for long tonight.

Finally, she left the restroom. Turning the corner, she ran headfirst into Rod. Stunned, she stepped back. "Oh, hi," her voice was unenthusiastic and she immediately cursed herself silently.

Rod seemed taken back. He did not understand why she was not happy to see him. Shrugging it off mentally, he leaned forward and kissed her. Her lips were cool and unresponsive against his. "What's wrong? And what are you doing here, Tricia?"

Awkwardly, Tricia shrugged. "I'm fine. I just came here with an old friend. What brings you here tonight?"

Rod motioned toward the refreshments counter. "Just getting some drinks for an out-of-town developer and me." He waited awkwardly for a moment and started to leave. Before he could, John walked up and handed Tricia a Sprite.

"Sorry about the Sprite, I ordered coke. For some reason, that is not what they heard." Stretching out his hand to Rod, he smiled affably. "Hi, I'm John. How are you doing?"

Rod coughed. He did not like the way this situation looked. Raising an eyebrow, he shook John's hand. "I'm Rod, Tricia's boyfriend. What brings you to town?"

John smiled. "Business, like always." Now he knew who the competition was.

Glancing over at Tricia's silent face, Rod frowned. "What type of business?"

Before John could respond, Tricia pulled at his arm. "We're headed back to the rodeo now. I'll call you tonight, Rod."

Rod leaned forward to kiss Tricia, but she moved so that the kiss fell on her cheek instead of her lips. Both men noticed this movement. Frowning, Rod walked away to get his drinks.

Returning to their seats, John poured another few shots of vodka into the sodas. "So that was Rod, huh? He's pretty good-looking."

Tricia shrugged. She did not like this conversation. Grabbing the cup from him, she downed all of the soda and liquor. "Let's get out of here. I don't want to talk about this."

John stood up. "Whatever you want. Any particular destination in mind?"

Tricia shook her head. "Let's just drive."

Getting on the roadway, they started to drive east. John was silent as he waited for Tricia to say something. Sitting next to him, Tricia just stared out the window. Things were already falling apart and nothing had happened. She could probably fix things with Rod fairly easy, but fixing her own emotions would be harder. It felt like she was standing at a precipice and looking over. If she decided to leap off the edge, she would be unable to change her mind in the future.

Finally, she looked over at John. Pulling out the vodka, she took a swig. John raised an eyebrow. "You kept the rest of the bottle?"

Tricia handed it to him. Sighing, he took a gulp. Noticing a side road, he turned off. Over the last few minutes, they had managed to drive out of the DFW metropolis and were on country lanes. The road they turned onto had no houses in sight. Some oak trees hid their car from the main road as they parked in an empty meadow.

Tricia glanced at John in surprise. "Why did we stop?" she asked.

"If you want to drink, we need to stop driving. I can always call a cab from here later. GPS should make it easy enough for the cab to find us."

Sighing, Tricia glanced at him. As she turned her face, her lips nearly hit his. She did not move a muscle and John remained frozen. Only a centimeter away from his mouth, her lips quivered with anticipation. Long moments passed, but neither person moved closer to the other. Within the car, the sexual tension became thick enough to cut with a knife.

Coughing, John moved his head back. He pulled out the vodka bottle and took another swig. "You are playing a dangerous game here. Maybe I should take you home. If you don't want anything to happen, I'll make sure you get home safe and with a clean conscious."

Silent, Tricia leaned back and closed her eyes. Images of John's body flashed across her mind. In her mental eye, he was behind her and thrusting inside of her. His hands ripped her clothes off. Sighing in frustration, she opened her eyes again. John was still sitting next to her and waiting for her to say something.

Perhaps it was the alcohol or the last year of grief. Whatever caused it, Tricia suddenly felt reckless. Pulling his keys out of the ignition, she tossed them in the backseat. She slid her leg over the top of him and straddled his body. Unquestioning, John pushed his seat farther away from the steering wheel. He waited for her to make a move—he did not want to push her into anything.

Tricia ran her tongue over her lips. Seductively, she leaned forward and whispered into his ear. "Don't kiss me."

Slowly, she brought her lips against his. Only a hair's breadth away from his, he could feel her breath against the soft skin of his mouth. Moving her lips so they remained almost touching his body, she allowed them to trace the outside of his ear and the line of his neck. Beneath her, she could feel John trembling in desire. With only the thin material of his slacks and the lace of her underwear between them, she could easily feel his cock harden against hers. The very thought of him inside her made her maddeningly wet. She wanted to touch him and stroke him, but could not bring herself to break this spell. As long as her lips did not touch his and they did nothing physical, she was not cheating on Rod yet.

She ran her hand along her collarbone and played with her nipple. Beneath the thin black lace of her bra, her nipple visibly hardened. John groaned and thrust his hips upward. With so little fabric between them, his cock rubbed against her clit. Noticing her response, he did it again. Breaking the spell slightly, he grabbed her hips and pulled them hard against him. The stimulation to her clit drove her wild. All she wanted was for him to be inside of her.

John could not stand it anymore. His teeth found her ear and he nibbled along the edge teasingly. Tricia looked down at him in surprise. "But I thought..." she started to say.

Before she could finish her sentence, John pulled her mouth down against his. His tongue moved against hers in a rhythm that she knew very well. Within her, it felt like fireworks or shooting stars were exploding in quick succession. She did not care anymore. Faithful or not, she did not care about anything. All that existed for her in this moment was the thought of John with her and inside of her. Yanking at his belt, she unbuttoned his pants so his throbbing member could break free. Long and hard, it was already dripping pre-cum with anticipation and desire. Slipping off her underwear, she straddled him. John reached for the glove box for a condom, but she pushed him away. If she did not have him now, she would explode with pent-up desire.

The lips of her cunt teased invitingly around his head. He could feel each nuance of her and the wetness that was beginning to surround him. With one quick thrust, he entered her. Again and again in quick succession, he allowed the entirety of his shaft to penetrate her body. Pain and pleasure intermingled in her mind as she cried out. Her screams of pleasure sounded like something out of an ancient mating ritual or an old harvest celebration. Her female nature invited him in as a part of something that had existed since the beginning of time. With each thrust, her body became his and he likewise became a part of her. They were no longer separate beings, but one soul rocking with fervor in his car. The windows fogged up as she moved her hips hard against his. Bringing him close to orgasm, she slowed down again and again to drag him away from the brink. Again, she moved her hips fervently and harshly against his. By the third time John approached orgasm, she could not take it any more. She had to come with him. That was the only way that this desire and union of their souls could be completed. Throwing back her head, she moaned loudly as she came around him.

As she left the pinnacle of her orgasm, Tricia realized it was not enough. She wanted him in every way possible. Just having sex would not be enough tonight. Kissing him passionately, she poured another shot down his throat as she drank an additional shot. She pulled him out of the car and bent over against it. Her long legs rose in a sleek line out of her cowboy boots. With her dress pulled up from sex, the line of her bottom was visible beneath the dress. Behind her, John was sexily tousled. His shirt had come unbuttoned during sex and his hair was a blond swirl around his head. Ripping off his shirt and undershirt, he exposed his naked muscles to the open night air. He no longer cared if anyone drove by and saw him. In his eyes, lust shone through and danger lurked. Stripping off his boxers, he put his manhood against her backside.

"What do you want?" John asked. His voice was strained as he tried to hold his body back from continuing.

Tricia shrugged. "I want you in every way possible. Use me however you want."

John did not need to be told a second time. He touched himself and felt her wetness still around his cock. Using moisture from his mouth, he wet the head further before entering her anally. Unwarned, Tricia cried out. The first instant of pain quickly subsided and she felt a new, different type of desire. Unlike typical sex, this sensation was entirely different. To her surprise, it was not unpleasant. Actually, she liked it. Pushing backward into him, she helped him thrust harder.

The added tightness around him brought John closer to orgasm than he had thought possible this soon. Reaching around to her chest, he fondled her breasts as he attempted to slow the almost compulsive thrusting of his hips. Instead of calming him down, the softness of her breasts and hard nipples made him even harder. Groaning in agony, he leaned back and placed his hands against her hips. Pulling her into him roughly, he tried to get the full length of his shaft inside. Frustrated by his inability to fit fully within her, he tried thrusting again. The tightness just teased him and brought him closer to orgasm without full satisfaction. Moaning in agony again, he ripped her from the car and threw her to ground. Tricia started to say something, but he held his hand over her mouth. There was no way he could stop even for a moment.

Entering her cunt again, he sighed in pleasure as he managed to fit his entire shaft within her. Tricia's wrists hurt slightly as he held her down. His weight was crushing her body, but she just wanted more. Free to talk at last, she whispered, "Hit me."

Without thinking about it, John pulled his hand back and slapped her. Although she did not understand why, this turned her on immensely. She nodded to him again. "Hit me. Harder."

John hit her again. As she started to tell him to hit her even harder, he placed both of his hands around her neck and choked her. The sudden lack of oxygen stimulated her nerves and allowed her to feel each part of her body as he thrust. Nodding her head and unable to speak, her eyes urged him on. John choked her again. Pulling one hand down from her neck, he fondled her clit. The extra stimulation brought her close to orgasm. Choking and unable to call out, she let out a silent moan as her body shook with her orgasm. Like an earthquake or tsunami, the orgasm passed over her body and caused convulsions within every fiber of her muscles. Above her, John started to orgasm for the second time of the night. Sighing in pleasure, he collapsed next to her.

Rolling against his body, she leaned her head on his chest. He lazily traced his hand along her back. Within moments, they were both fast asleep and naked in each other's arms.

Minutes or hours later, Tricia woke up. For a second, she was confused. Around her was just woodlands and prairie. Looking over, she saw John and groaned. She had tried to resist for at least a while, but resistance was apparently impossible. Sitting up, she shook some leaves off of her arm that had fallen during the night. Next to her, John began to stir.

Opening his eyes, he smiled when he saw her there. Pulling her back into his arms, he kissed the top of her head. "You are amazing, you know," he paused. "Does this mean that you are going to leave Rod?"

Tricia shook her head. In addition to the beginnings of a hangover, she knew she had to sort out the confusion of her life. "No. Or I don't know. You know that it doesn't make any sense for us to be together."

John shrugged. "When does love make sense? Come on, you can't tell me that you experience that attraction or level of sex every day."

Glaring at him, Tricia reached for her underwear. "I don't choose who I am with based on sex." John laughed at how cute her angry expression looked. "Well, it is a factor. For good sex, two people have to be compatible. So it at least indicates something of a non-physical nature." Pulling on her dress, Tricia motioned to the car. "Come on, drive me home. I'll call and tell you how this all works out."

Nodding, he walked to the car and opened her door. "Fair enough, let's go."

Silent again, Tricia got in the car and stared out the window until he dropped her off. How would she possibly explain this to Rob?

Chapter Two

Still a little unsteady on her feet, Tricia turned the key in her door and waved John off. Entering the darkened house, she dropped her purse in the living room. As she turned, her mind processed the shadows in the room. She realized that someone was there. Reaching for the light switch, she turned it on. Rod was sitting there. He was bleary-eyed from waiting so many hours for her to return home. Tricia stood there silently and stared at him.

Taking her disheveled appearance in, he raised an eyebrow. His voice was cool and showed the effort he was making to remain calm. "Who... was... that...?" he spoke evenly and slowly.

Tricia shrugged. There was no point in lying. What he could not guess on his own, her appearance would show. "I was with John."

"Did you sleep with him? Who is he?" The strain of the pain he was filling slipped out as his voice broke. He ran his fingers through his hair.

Tricia nodded. "Yes. I did. He is my former boss."

Standing up, Rod walked over to the window. "You never told me that you guys were," he paused and spat out the remaining words, "romantically involved."

Tricia shrugged. "I wasn't ready to say anything. Last night was not supposed to happen." She tried to shift her feet so that she could see his expression. Frozen in place, Rod just continued to stare out the window.

"Not supposed to happen? I thought you were with me. Hell, I was thinking about marrying you someday. Without telling me where you were going, who you were with or your history with him, you went off with this guy."

Tricia did not say anything. There were no excuses and she deserved this.

Returning to the couch, Rod sat down. "Do you love him?"

Uncertain what to say, Tricia did not say anything. Rod looked at her again. Judgment was in his eyes.

"Do you love him?" he asked her again. His voice was sharp and hid the anger that was boiling within him.

Gazing straight into Rod's eyes, Tricia kept her face emotionless as she lied. "No."

Rod's arm jerked outward and hit a vase. The sound of it crashing against the wall startled both of them. For the first time, Tricia started to feel afraid. Rod stood up and strode confidently across the room. Pushing her against the wall, he stopped her from turning away from him. Beneath his arms, she could already feel painful bruises starting to form.

"Don't lie to me," he hissed. "Do you love him?"

She nodded slowly. Until this moment, she had not been completely sure of her feelings. She did love John. At the same time, she was starting to love Rod. Until this outburst, he had proven himself to be the man she was searching for.

Moments passed as Rod gazed at her in rage. He did not throw anything or make any movements. Instead, it seemed like he was using all of his willpower to control himself. As the threat of violence passed, Tricia squirmed and tried to get away. Inexplicably, the writhing of her body caught his attention. Sudden desire flushed through his body as he remembered their first time in the Dallas hotel.

Grabbing her arms, he threw her down onto the floor. Grabbing her mother's letter opener from the desk, he held her dress tightly and cut it in a straight line down the front. Her smooth cocoa breast popped out invitingly and her dark nipples hardened enticingly for him. Groaning, he ran the letter opener down her body. The sharp thrill of his knife caused her hairs to stand on end. With the rage of just a moment ago, she feared that he would cut her. At the same time, she already wanted him. Tonight, it seemed like her desire was completely unbridled. For the first time in her life, she would sleep with two men in the same night.

Gliding the letter opener down to his legs, he pulled at the lace of her underwear and cut it in a clean motion. Rod tossed the letter opener to the side and stripped off his shirt. His rippling pecs shone in the dim light as he spread her legs. Placing a finger inside of her, he felt how wet she was. His eyes opened as he realized that it would be impossible for all of the wetness to be from her. Rod felt rage burning again within his chest. If John could have sex and come inside of her, he would do the same.

Pulling off his pants, he prepared to enter her. Tricia tried to push him away for a second as she realized that he was not going to put on protection. "Wait," she said, but he cut her off.

"You let some random guy do this. Why not me? I'm your boyfriend." His voice was filled with anger and hurt. Weakly, Tricia leaned back against the ground and let him enter her. The violent thrust was unlike anything she had ever felt. It was as if he wanted her to experience the pain that he was feeling. Despite the intense pain that accompanied each thrust, she found herself experiencing a sensation of pleasure. The smooth skin of his cock barely fit inside her and each thrust was accompanied by a wide range of sensations.

Rod thrust again. His rage was gradually being driven away by desire. Her lithe body moved against his and accepted him deeper inside of her. Pulling her onto his lap, he caressed the soft skin of her breasts and pulled her nipple into his mouth. The pleasure was excruciatingly sweet and he wanted more. On top of him, Tricia thrust her hips down onto his. With each thrust, he filled her completely and drove her desire into a frenzy. Moving rapidly now, she could not bring herself to stop. She had to have him in her. Across from them, the open window started to let in the first rays of sunshine. People walking by would see them, but she did not care. Even if the whole world was watching her right now, she would not stop.

Moaning with agony, she wrapped her legs tightly around his hips. His abs contracted as he strove to push further into her. Biting into his shoulder, she tried to muffle a scream as she felt herself begin to orgasm. The delicious contractions of her cunt teased and tantalized him mercilessly as he finally started to approach orgasm. Crying out, he came with her and pulled her body into his.

As desire faded, Rod uncomfortably moved to pull on his pants. He had not intended to sleep with her and had actually planned on breaking up with her tonight. This was unacceptable to him, but he could not help it. Her sensual, provocative curves were too enticing to resist. Hell, he had almost raped her in his unbridled passion. Blushing, he looked over at her to see if she was okay.

Next to him, Tricia sat stunned on the floor. The afterglow from sex was slowly drifting away and she realized what an unusual position she was in. Deciding to deal with this later, she shrugged her shoulders. She needed to get a glass of water or her headache would be unbelievably terrible. Standing up, the shreds of her dress and lace underwear fell to the ground. Her warm, chocolate skin gleamed with the glow of sweat and sex.

Across the room, Rod watched her. Each of her curves flowed smoothly into her long, athletic legs. Her full lips were matched by a flat stomach that drove him wild just to think about it. Without consciously thinking about what he was doing, he reached down and touched himself. Already, he was standing straight up. So much for controlling himself. As she poured a glass of water, he stripped his clothes off and strode into the kitchen.

Positioning his muscular legs behind her, he pressed against her from behind.

Surprised, Tricia turned. "I thought you were still angry at me. What are you trying to do?"

Rod wrapped his arms around her and held her close. He could smell the sweet scent of jasmine and lilacs on her body. "I have no clue what I am doing. My whole life, I have made the rational decision. I went to college to get out of the ghetto and got a real estate license to make money. Right now, I am doing the most irrational thing possible. Yet... I love you. I am attracted to you like I have never been to anyone. And if you let me, I would take you again right on the kitchen table."

Smiling, Tricia turned to face him. His member brushed against her stomach as she turned and she could feel the hardness of each muscle in his body. "Take me then," she said simply without explanation.

It only took a word from her to release his pent-up energy again. Throwing her stomach on the table, he entered her from behind. The instant sensation of pleasure was intense for both of them. With each thrust, he hit her G-spot with an unbelievably intense force. Arching her back, she pushed her hips deeper onto him. Every time she glanced back, the sight of his muscles bulging and straining against her only turned her on more.

Grasping on the front of the kitchen table, she used her grip to help her propel her hips into his. The sudden movement caught him off guard. With the sudden pleasure, he orgasmed. Gasping, he fell against her body. The heat of his body against hers felt wonderful.

Turning onto her back, she wrapped her legs around him and pulled him onto the kitchen table on top of her. Pushing him back inside her, she enjoyed the feeling of him within her. If only life could always be like this. In this moment, there was no confusion and just raw pleasure.

Rod sighed. Propping his head up on her breasts, he gazed into her eyes. Still inside her, he was finding it difficult to focus entirely. Although desire still remained, it had dimmed and his anger had evaporated. "What are you going to do, Tricia?" he asked.

Lovingly, Tricia stroked the top of his head and rocked her hips against his playfully. "I really don't know. I thought everything was over with John or I wouldn't have started a relationship with you. At the same time, I find myself falling for you. I've never been in a situation like this before and I don't know what to do."

Rod kissed the palm of her hand gently. "Do you love me?"

Tricia nodded. "At least, I'm starting to."

Sighing, Rod thrust deeply inside of her. His cock quivered and he felt a sudden urge to have sex again. Ignoring it, he pulled out of her with a sigh. Standing up, he let her see the full length of his body. The visible admiration in his eyes made him smile. "Well, Tricia. Tell me what you want to do. I will wait however long as you want for a decision. No strings attached. If you want to date me in the end, I am fine with that. If you want to marry me, I would also love for that to happen. You just have to tell me what you want and I will do it."

Nodding, Tricia stood up and walked him to get his clothes. Before leaving the house, he put on his clothes. Tricia remained naked. No one would be able to see her in the entryway and she liked the appreciative looks she was getting from Rod.

At the front door, she gave him a long kiss goodbye. "I'll call you, Rod, and let you know." He nodded in response and turned almost sadly away. Rod knew that this could be the last time that he saw her or their life together. The momentous significance of this brief parting floored him. He just hoped that she made the right choice.

Chapter Three

Sitting alone in her bedroom, Tricia smoked a cigarette. She had bought the pack after her mother died, but only smoked one cigarette out of it. Tricia never smoked, but right now seemed like the time to start. She had no clue what to do. Everything felt right with John, but they got glares from older people whenever they went out. Rod was the right choice on paper. He was successful and caring. Although the moment of anger had scared her at the time, the circumstances were unlikely to ever occur again. Leaning back, she let the cool air from the window blow across her body. She had not bothered to put on clothes and the chilly air caused her skin to form goose bumps.

Tricia began to pace the room as she finished the cigarette. She tried to imagine life without John or without Rod. When she realized that one of these options was impossible, she knew what to do. Immediately, she went to take a shower and sleep. She would need her rest by tomorrow.

Tricia waited through security in anticipation. The flight had seemed impossibly long as her excitement level grew. She had no clue how John would react to seeing her. She had thought about calling him in the last week, but had not wanted to ruin her surprise. In her mind, she imagined him sweeping her off her feet and carrying her to bed.

Finally getting into a taxi, she gave the driver the address to John's house. Staring out the window in thought, time suddenly sped up. Before long, she was at his house. Accustomed to entering through the servant's entrance, she walked by the same guards that she had greeted each day that she had worked here. Although surprised to see her, the guards waved her on.

Entering through the kitchen, she caught sight of Stuart, the chef. "Hey, Tricia! What brings you up here?" He motioned to the kitchen table. "Sit down and stay a while."

Tricia shook her head. "I have to talk to John. We'll talk later and catch up, okay?"

Stuart nodded knowingly. "I understand. I always thought there was something between you."

Startled, Tricia glanced back at him. "You knew?"

Shaking his head, Stuart lowered his voice. His demeanor was friendly. "It's okay, love knows no bounds. Plus, John had gone through enough. Having a moment of happiness was good for him." He motioned toward the door to the mansion. "Go ahead. Go see him."

Nodding in assent, Tricia climbed the stairs and walked through the hallways of the house. At John's office door, she paused. Summoning her courage, she entered the room quietly. Inside, John was sitting at his desk with his head in his hands. She stood there for a moment before saying a quiet "hello".

Looking up, John caught sight of her. He stood immediately from the desk and rushed to her. Grabbing her in his arms, he locked her in an embrace. Stepping back, he kneeled on one knee.

"Tricia, you are the woman that I want to spend my life with. When you are with me, the whole world stops and all I see or care about is you. Be with me. Marry me." He kissed her hand.

Stunned, Tricia said the only thing she could think of. "How did you know to buy the ring?"

John shrugged. "I just hoped that you would come. I've been carrying it around for the last week in the hope that you would come," he paused. "So... will you marry me?"

Tricia nodded and pulled him up from his kneeling position. "Yes, yes, I will marry you."

-The End-

If you enjoyed this series, I would appreciate your leaving a review of the book. Good reviews encourage an author to write as well as help books to sell. Good reviews can be just a few short sentences describing what you liked about the book without having a spoiler. If you could spend 30 seconds writing a review, I would appreciate it: you can review this title right now at your favorite retailer.

Here is a preview of **another story** you may enjoy:

Love Disrupted - Ardent Billionaire Romance Series, Book 1

DEIRDRE CLARKE stepped out of her apartment into the hot Los Angeles sun; dusk had fallen, but the temperature still sat near 100 degrees. Deirdre was already running late for her gig, so the sight of her ex-boyfriend Carl standing by her car irritated her even more than usual. She stomped down the single flight of stairs and greeted him with hostility.

"I'm late. What the hell do you want?" Deirdre demanded.

"Can't a man just stop by to see his best girl?" Carl smiled. His green eyes complimented his mocha skin and for a moment Deirdre forgot why she'd put up with his shit for so long. Then she remembered why she'd stopped.

"I guess you'd better go see her then," she said roughly. "And let me be on my way."

"Dee… you know I'm talking about you."

"I'm not your girl no more," she answered, "and I've got somewhere to be."

"Don't be mad, Dee I just came here to check on you… you alright? What about D'Angelo? You two need anything? You got rent covered?"

Deirdre's blood boiled and she met his eyes with a defiant stare. "I don't need a damn thing from you. D'Angelo and I are not your business anymore." Deirdre had been responsible for her younger brother since their mother had gone to prison. D'Angelo was one of the reasons she'd known she had to get away from Carl in the first place. The last thing she wanted was for her brother to see her thug ex-boyfriend as a role model.

"When are you going to understand that you can't buy your way back here?" She glared at him.

"Deirdre, we were together almost our whole lives. I love you. But I'm not trying to buy my way back. I have a business proposition for you."

"I don't need a job, I have two," she snapped, trying to open her car door. Carl blocked her way.

"Its easy money Dee… you wouldn't even know it was here."

"Ah, I see. You think I'll hide drugs or hot shit for you, after all of the hell you put me through? You think I'd take that risk for you and your 'boys'?" She snorted back at him.

"It's just herb, Dee… it's practically legal. And I don't know why you're so pissed at me. Nothing that went down was my FAULT!"

"Our windows were SHOT OUT, Carl. You can stand there all you want and claim it was a random drive-by, swear it wasn't personal, but I'm not a moron! You think I didn't know you'd fallen in with Derrick and his thugs? You think I believed your lies about where all the money was coming from? I KNEW what you were doing, and you just denied, denied, denied. Until our home was shot up... with my brother inside. Take your shit and get out of my face." Deirdre shoved him out of the way of her car and escaped inside. She checked her face in the rearview mirror, and then prayed she'd have time to fix her make-up before she had to go onstage.

She stood on stage, in her element. As Lou played along on the black grand piano, Deirdre let all of her emotions flow out to the music. The small crowd gave her their undivided attention as she belted out Trouble, Stormy Weather, and Summertime. Her white, full length gown stood in stark contrast to the milk-chocolate color of her skin.

Deirdre couldn't remember a time when she didn't love to sing. When she was still a young girl, before her father left, her family went to church every Sunday. She loved listening to the soloists in the choir and dreamed of one day standing next to them. But they'd stopped going to church once her father was gone. When D'Angelo was born, Deirdre had tried to get her mother to go back, but she'd refused; D'Angelo's father was against the idea. But soon, he was gone too. Looking back, Deirdre was sure that was when her mother started using drugs, though she didn't realize what was happening at the time. Three years ago, right after Deirdre graduated from high-school, Pauline Clarke had been busted and sentenced to twenty years in a federal prison. Deirdre became D'Angelo's legal guardian, though in all honesty she'd raised him since he was born.

D'Angelo was a good kid, especially considering everything he'd been through. And he was the reason Deirdre hadn't fallen into the same kind of traps the other girls in her neighborhood had found themselves in. She hadn't had any kids, she hadn't gotten messed up on drugs, and she didn't take her clothes off for money. Instead, Deirdre worked as a hotel maid and took college courses online. She'd have loved to go to school on an actual campus, but she couldn't afford childcare for D'Angelo and she refused to turn him into a latchkey kid at eight years old. Deirdre worked while he was at school, and then after dinner they did their homework together.

Thursday nights were different. Those nights were all for Deirdre. She had a standing gig at Fuseli's, an upscale jazz club in the Hollywood foothills. The gig paid just enough for Deirdre to afford her stage-clothes, but she didn't do it for the money.

When she finished her last set, Deirdre took a seat at the bar and ordered herself a beer and a sandwich. As the bartender walked towards the tap, a tall, broad stranger signaled his attention. When he returned to Deirdre, he carried a martini with her draft.

"Dee, a kind gentleman asked me to bring you this and wondered if you'd mind some company?"

Deirdre looked up at Steve and sighed. After her encounter with Carl, she was in no mood to put up with anyone's advances. "Tell him thank you, but I can't possibly accept."

"I don't know… this one's pretty hot, Dee… he's the one down there, in the suit."

"Really Steve, I'm not up for it right now."

"Alright, fine…" he answered in a disapproving, sing-song voice.

Deirdre thought the issue was dealt with as she watched Steve approach the end of the bar to deliver the message. The gorgeous blonde man took the martini, rose, and headed Deirdre's way.

"I'm sorry," she began as he approached, frustrated that he wouldn't take a hint.

"No, I'm sorry." He smiled. "Your friend told me you've had a bad day. You sang beautifully… I sent this as a token of my appreciation, nothing more," he explained, raising the drink. "Why don't you enjoy it? It might make you feel better. Or I could buy you something else, if you'd prefer? Right before I return to my seat, of course."

If you enjoyed this sample then look for **Love Disrupted - Ardent Billionaire Romance Series, Book 1.**

Here is a preview of **another story** you may enjoy:

"**EXHALE SLOWLY**," the yoga instructor said in a soothing voice. Alexandra exhaled her breath and relaxed her muscles. As she exhaled, she consciously focused on releasing all of her worries. Her body was in the bridge pose, so her navel faced the twirling ceiling fan.

"Inhale through your nose," came the second instruction. Alexandra inhaled and the sound of her breath filled her ears. She held the pose for what seemed like a lifetime as the base of her neck pressed against the floor.

"Release," came the blessed instruction, finally. Automatically, Alexandra moved into corpse pose. She had been practicing yoga for three months and was finally feeling confident about her poses. She knew that there was still a long way to go, but she was getting there. Her mind was relaxed as she felt the warm caress of the sunlight travel along her torso. A smile spread across her face as she focused on existing entirely in the moment. Without thought, she moved fluidly between all of the yoga positions.

Her eyes opened and her mind returned when the instructor ended the session, "Thank you for attending, *Namaste*."

"*Namaste*," Alexandra replied with her palms together. As she rolled up her mat, she looked around at the other patrons. All were covered in sweat, all wearing modern yoga shorts and tops. Only the instructor wore the loose-fitting, traditional clothes of

Kundalini yoga. Karen, the instructor, stood at the head of the class in conversation with a few of the patrons.

Turning away from everyone else, Alexandra studied her figure in the large mirror that lined the wall of the room. Her eyes wandered across her own body and she felt pleasure at seeing the results of her many yoga sessions. The pink and black yoga pants fit perfectly along her dark calves and hips. Slender, yet toned, she admired her own hourglass figure in the mirror. Her eyes glanced at her glistening ebony skin and the few beads of sweat that dotted her skin from the overly warm room. She released her curly hair from the clasp of a bun and watched as it cascaded down her shoulders.

With a broad smile, she turned to leave the room. She walked toward the door and placed her hand on the warm metal doorknob. As the door pushed forward, she looked over her shoulder to say goodbye to her instructor. She noticed Karen and a man speaking with each other, their eyes looking at Alexa's toned figure. Dismissing the glances, she turned away with a cheery wave.

A few blocks down the street was her favorite café, the one that she went to after yoga class. As she walked there, she could feel the eyes of other people watching her—mostly men. Not long ago after making a steady income, she had moved to a more upscale segment of town. As one of the few African-Americans in town, she drew stares that ranged from curious to desirous whenever she went out. She did not mind the ogling, but it was the catcalls that ate at her. Catcalls were so vulgar and seemed cowardly. If someone wanted to speak to her, then she would prefer that they were up front with her. She felt that a real man would be one who says what he means and does not just yell something out of a speeding car window.

If you enjoyed this sample then look for **Love Reserved: Fervent Billionaire BWWM Romance Series, Book 1**.

Here is a preview of **another story** you may enjoy:

Love Deceived: Tenacious Billionaire BWWM Romance Series, Book 1

"**I LIKE** your buns." The customer's voice was creamy, with a hint of spice. "How much are they?"

"Excuse me?" Adalia glanced up from behind the cash register and glared at the man.

"Your buns," he answered, flashing a naughty grin at her.

Heat erupted in her core.

It was him. The guy. He came in every day in that Prada suit, no suitcase, and flaunted his perfect jawline and wavy blond hair. Adalia's stomach did a turn, but she steadied herself mentally.

Come on, it's just a customer. Same as any other in the bakery.

"Can I help you with something?" She asked the same question each day when he came in. Then it would begin.

"That depends." The gorgeous man strolled over and rested his elbows on the glass of the counter that displayed treats and sweets.

"On what, exactly? It's pretty simple," she answered. "Either you want the buns or you don't."

"Oh," he replied, interlocking his fingers and resting his chin on them. "I want the buns. You can count on that." He reached out and brushed her forearm with the tips of his fingers. Sparks danced across her ebony skin.

Adalia cleared her throat gently, but didn't move away. It was the first time he'd touched her, and she'd honestly fantasized about the moment for weeks.

"Which buns would you like?" She breathed the words, and he leaned in close enough that she caught a whiff of his cologne. It was a masculine, woody scent and it suited him perfectly.

Warning alarms went off in her head – this guy was clearly a player, well put together, with that easy charm – but they were drowned out by her attraction to him.

"Yours," he uttered, "every day, for the next month. Every night, too."

Adalia narrowed her chocolate brown eyes at him. She'd given up trusting anyone a long time ago, let alone suave white strangers with a clear desire for more than a carb fix.

"I wouldn't advise you eat that many carbs. And you've yet to specify which type of buns you'd like, sir." She gave a sweet smile she didn't feel in her gut.

Why couldn't she shake her attraction to this guy? She'd just gotten out of a relationship with DeShawn, just started the healing process. She had to focus on getting the bakery on track, not on some sexy dude with a fetish for curvy women.

God, wouldn't it be nice if he had a fetish for – No!

He studied her expression with a grin that made her insides go melty like tempered chocolate.

"I think you know which buns I want."

"Cinnamon," she answered, reaching over for a brown paper bag beneath the glass fronted cabinet. In the back, one of her bakers slammed a tray in the oven and cursed.

Irritation flickered through her – they never treated those ovens with respect – but she kept a straight face.

"No, no," he answered, then grasped her wrist again, and heat waves assaulted her. "I'm in the mood for chocolate today."

She stared him dead in the eye, willing the arousal to back the hell down. "Smooth," she said wryly.

"Excuse me, miss. I'd like to pay?" said a hunched over granny, clasping a box of éclairs.

"Sorry, ma'am," Adalia replied, sparing a frown for the handsome businessman. He winked a blue eye at her and she swallowed hard. "That will be five dollars."

"Five dollars," the lady answered, squinting a little and stretching to pat her curlers. Adalia glanced at 'Handsome Guy' again. He hadn't looked away, and their gazes were glued for a moment. "I'll tell you, it's a pity these éclairs are so good, dearie. You're going to have me on the streets at this rate."

"I'm glad you like them," Adalia replied. That was the plain truth: with the bills piling up, every happy customer helped pave the pathway to financial success. Losing her lifelong dream wasn't an option. "Can I get you anything else?"

"Oh no, dear. Perhaps the recipe so I can make these for myself at home." The old woman's wrinkled façade split into a friendly smile. "No, I'm joking, of course. I quite enjoy the trip into the city for these treasures." She lifted one from the bag and took a bite. Cream squished out the sides and smeared onto her cheek.

"I'll get you a napkin." Adalia fumbled for them beside the register, but Handsome Guy was already on it.

He swept out a handkerchief and handed it to the customer with a courteous bob of his head.

"Thank you," the lady breathed, accepting it with a flutter of her eyelids. "My, what a dashing young fellow. You certainly are a lucky woman." She directed that at Adalia.

"What? He's not my –"

"Not as lucky as I am," he put in, and gestured for the customer to keep the soft square of linen. She thanked him and shuffled out with a cheery wave, pink slippers slapping on the linoleum.

Adalia had given the bakery a fifties' style look. She'd loved the idea of a parlor where customers could sit and have a milkshake while they ate their baked goods. So far, the idea hadn't taken off.

The booths and chairs were empty. A pang of regret stabbed at her stomach, and she wiped down her flowered apron with a grimace.

"I'll get those chocolate buns for you," she said to the businessman, but the stare he gave her made her stop dead in her tracks. "What is it? You don't want them anymore?"

"I do, but I'd prefer it if you had a few with me. Do you make coffee here?"

"We do," she said, "but I've got way too much to do to take a break."

"I wasn't asking."

"Look, I don't even know your name. What makes you think you can come in here, flirt with me and make a fool out of me in front of my customers?" Adalia allowed anger to gutter through her and override the desperate need to reach out and spank that cute butt. "Now, if you want buns, I'll give you buns, but I'm going to have to ask you to leave."

"I assume you don't normally treat your customers this way." He glanced left and right, searching the empty storefront with mock intrigue.

"How I treat my customers is none of your business," she snapped. He'd hit a nerve there. The bakery was her life, her dream and her future, and it was falling through her fingers so fast, she barely had time to jam them shut.

Sunlight filtered through the front window, highlighting the golden streaks in his hair.

Adalia turned her back on him and got the damn chocolate buns, then thrust them at him over the counter. He took out a leather wallet with a flourish and flipped it open, but she shook her finger at him.

"No," she said, "these are free of charge."

"That's nice of you," he said, his left eyebrow lifted, and she longed to smack him in it. Then kiss him. Kiss him all over.

"It's free of charge because I don't consider you a customer. Don't come back here again. Understand?" She folded her arms and steadied her breathing.

The devilishly attractive businessman ran his thumb down his jaw, holding the brown bag aloft. "Sorry," he said, without a smidgen of the remorse he professed, "but I'm not in the habit of making promises I can't keep."

"Get out," she hissed at him.

He strolled to the door with a low chuckle and pulled it open with a tinkle of the bell. "I'll see you tomorrow, Adalia."

"How did you know my –?"

But he didn't let her finish, cutting across her with one word. It cut her to ribbons, zigzagged through the air between them on vibrations of smoldering need.

"Trent."

Then he was gone.

If you enjoyed this sample then look for **Love Deceived: Tenacious Billionaire BWWM Romance Series, Book 1.**

Here is a preview of **another book** you may also enjoy:

"THEY'RE ASKING for the eggs to be cooked again."

"What? Those are fine!"

"What do you want me to do about it, Brad? The customer is complaining. Just make them again, alright? He wants the eggs overcooked, apparently."

Brad took the plate from Stacey's hand and returned to his grill, grumbling loudly. Stacey wiped the sweat from her brow and turned around, getting ready to head back out onto the floor of *Papa's Grill and Diner*.

It was the middle of the day in mid-summer, which made the sweltering kitchen unbearable. Stacey was glad to leave the kitchen even if it meant dealing with a couple of jerk customers.

Back in the dining area, she looked around. She had only one couple in her section. They were older, with their shoulders hunched over and beady eyes pointed toward the kitchen. The woman hadn't touched her sandwich, probably waiting for the man to get his eggs back before digging in.

There was only one other waitress, Maria, working, and she was in the corner, texting on her phone. Their place wasn't exactly the hot spot of the city to eat during the best of times. During mid-day, it was more like a graveyard.

The woman motioned for Stacey to come over. She clenched her jaw, exhaled slowly and got ready for whatever ridiculous request the woman was going to make. This couple had been a hassle from the moment they were seated.

"How can I help you?" she asked, plastering a smile on her face.

The woman scowled, "Where are my husband's eggs?"

"They're making him a fresh batch right now."

"Tell them to hurry up!" the woman snapped.

The husband sat there silently, playing with the edge of his napkin. But he nodded at Stacey as if to tell her he better get his eggs soon.

Stacey scurried back into the kitchen. It was mind-numbing if she let it get to her. How long had she been working here now? Four years? It was supposed to be a pit stop before she moved onto bigger and better things. She had been there, scraping by, instead of returning to college or working on making something more of herself.

No use in thinking about that now.

Brad handed her a plate of freshly cooked eggs. She walked back to the table and placed it in front of the man and his wife.

The man wrinkled his nose and said, "This will do, I suppose."

Stacey clasped her hands together and inquired as politely as she could muster, "Would you like more coffee?"

They grunted, and she gave them a fresh pot, making sure not to add it their bill. She was sure they would want something for free out of the egg fiasco. By the time the couple left, Stacey was ready for a break.

In the break room, she slipped off her shoes and rubbed her feet, wincing. Her shoes were cheap, and it showed after standing in them for more than a couple of hours. Her feet were killing her.

She checked her phone next. There was a voicemail from her sister. It was a rare event that her sister reached out to her and she was filled with dread listening to the message.

"Stacey, hey. It's your sister, Allison," she added for clarification as if Stacey wouldn't know her own sister's name. "Listen, call me when you can? I have a question to ask you. Well, more of a favor? But I need to talk to you first. Thanks, bye."

Stacey sighed as the message ended. Her sister wanting a favor never led to anything good. *If she wants money, she can forget it.* There was no cash to give Allison. There were barely any funds for Stacey.

A small TV in the break room played the news. The image was grainy but she could just make out the weatherman talking about rain later on in the evening. *Great.* She made a mental note to make sure the roof didn't leak all over everything when she got home from work. Last time it stormed, Stacey had to set out buckets to catch the drips.

She closed her eyes just for a moment. If she left them closed for too long, she would fall asleep on the spot. It felt as if there was always something to do. She finished one thing, and another task popped up in its place. Maybe that was how it would always be.

"Wake up, sleepyhead."

Stacey opened her eyes to see Amanda stepping into the break room.

"You work today?" Stacey asked, surprised, wondering why they needed another waitress working during such a slow day.

"Nah, I left my wallet here last night in my locker. I was so tired after closing, it just slipped my mind." Amanda walked over to her locker and glanced back at Stacey. "You okay?"

"Yeah, just tired."

"Looks dead here. I'd be tired too," Amanda remarked as she opened up her locker.

"Yeah, it's pretty boring."

Amanda paused in front of her open locker, grabbed her wallet, and tucked it into her purse. When she turned back around, she had a strange look on her face. Stacey sat up straighter.

"What?"

Amanda hesitated and then sat down on the wooden bench. Stacey could see the purple circles under Amanda's eyes. Although they both worked full time at the restaurant, Amanda also attended college. She was probably just as tired as Stacey.

"I heard something. Probably just a rumor. I don't know. I wasn't going to tell anyone but—"

But I know how much you need this job was the unfinished thought there.

"What is it?"

Amanda lowered her voice, "Heard at a class yesterday this place might close down."

"Who was talking about that in your class?" Stacey scoffed. "Especially about our little place."

"Well, I mentioned that I work here. I was in my accounting class, and we were doing a project. This kid in my group said that I should look for other work because this place is going to shut down. Especially with all those investment groups coming in here trying to revive the area."

Stacey scowled. Her neighborhood, which was predominantly black, had indeed been crawling with rich white men in suits lately. All of them wanted to knock down and rebuild her section of town. They wanted to make it new and fresh again. They wanted it to appeal to the elite, which naturally meant getting rid of anyone who was low income.

"Thanks for the heads up, Amanda, but one kid in a college class saying we're going to close doesn't mean we are going to."

"Maybe. But this place is always dead. How long do you think we can stay open like this?" She stood up. "Don't tell anyone I told you, okay? I'll see you later."

Stacey watched her go, suddenly feeling wide awake. Even though she had sounded confident to Amanda that they weren't going to close, the girl had a point. Business had been awful lately. How long would they really be able to stay open?

Maybe it was time to find another job. The only reason Stacey had stuck around there for so long was how flexible the hours were. Few places would accommodate Stacey like that. But if this place was going to close, she may have to put some applications out.

She sighed and rubbed her forehead, fending off a headache. Just another worry to add to her long list.

If you enjoyed this sample then look for **Love Invested – Persuasive Billionaire BWWM Romance Series, Book 1**.

Other Books by Shyla Starr

- Persuasive Billionaire BWWM Romance Series

- Tenacious Billionaire BWWM Romance Series

- Elusive Billionaire Romance Series

- Ardent Billionaire Romance Series

- Fervent Billionaire BWWM Romance Series

- Audacious Billionaire BWWM Romance Series

Get the latest update on new releases from the author at:

https://shylastarr.com/newsletter/

About the Author - Shyla Starr

Shyla currently specializes in writing interracial romance stories and is a huge fan of the alpha male. Simply put, there just aren't enough stories about mixed couple romances, which is something she is aiming to fix.

Being a bookworm all her life, when Shyla discovered men she also realized how easy it was to fulfill her fantasies through her writing.

When not writing and fantasizing about men, Shyla enjoys dancing, reading and chilling with her friends.

Connect with Shyla Starr

I really appreciate you reading my book! Here are my social media coordinates:

Friend me on Facebook:
https://www.facebook.com/shylastarrauthor

Follow me on Twitter: https://twitter.com/shylstarr

Check me out on Goodreads:
https://www.goodreads.com/author/show/8436084.Shyl a_Starr

Subscribe to my newsletter:
https://shylastarr.com/newsletter/

Visit my website: https://shylastarr.com/

www.ingramcontent.com/pod-product-compliance
Lightning Source LLC
Chambersburg PA
CBHW030818200726
48288CB00004B/1281